IT'S CHRISTMAS AGAIN

BERNICE BLOOM

Bernice Bloom

FOREWORD

Hello Dear Readers,

Thank you so much for downloading IT'S CHRISTMAS AGAIN. I hope you enjoy a second Christmas with Mary Brown. You will recall, if you joined her for the first Christmas book, that she is not a lady to 'under-do' the festive season, and this year is no exception.

You'll see her back at the Beckhams' house again, determined that an elephant has a rightful place in the Christmas manger, and getting into the most astonishing trouble while organising a date, collecting sticks and receiving a present from a kindly customer.

I hope you enjoy it.

Lots of love,

BBx

THE 12 DAYS OF MARY'S MAD CHRISTMAS

On the twelfth day of Christmas, my true love sent to me:

* One stuffed elephant
    * One Christmas Post-Box
    * One lonely colleague ·
    * One Beckham tree
    * One pile of sticks
    * One crazy date
    * One remote control
    * One broken telly
    * One flight to Lapland
    * One sexy Viking
    * One little question
    * And a Mary who's very happy…

CHAPTER 1

15TH DECEMBER

'*I*t's Christmas tiiiiime....' I yell into Ted's ear, in the manner of Nodder Holder. He jumps as he wakes up and throws his big hands against his ears, muttering obscenities at me. Then he pulls the duvet over his head and turns away.

My words of seasonal joy haven't had quite the effect on my beloved that I hoped they might.

I guess most people would take this as a sign that he doesn't want to be disturbed, and walk away. Not me. I'm not perturbed. Oh no. Nothing can dampen the Christmas spirit that is soaring through my veins. I sit up and start singing *Twelve Days of Christmas*.

'On what planet is it Christmas today?' Ted shouts over the sound of my awful singing. 'It's 15th December. That's not Christmas Day anywhere.'

'No, not Christmas Day,' I say. 'It's Christmas time. This is the day that the count-down to Christmas starts at work. And you remember who's in charge of it all at work, don't you?'

There's a long sigh and a grumpy noise from the lump under the duvet.

'Meeeeeeee,' I remind him. I was 'in charge' of Christmas for the first-time last year, and it was an absolute triumph, even if I say so myself, so this year I'm back in the saddle.

Ted sits up and rubs his eyes.

'I can build my lovely nativity scene today and put up the magic *Post Box of Wishes and Dreams*. Also, we're going to start giving sweets out to all the children who come to the store which will be lovely.'

'Yeah well, I'd be a bit cautious about the handing out of sweets to children. That can end badly.'

'Nonsense,' I tell him, as I get changed for work. This morning I don't have to clamber into the terrible green uniform that makes me look like a cross between Kermit and Shrek. No, no – I'm not working on the tills for the next 12 days, I'm leading festive marketing until December 27th, so I put on my red Christmas jumper with big holly leaves on the front. The great joy of this jumper is that, in addition to the fact that it has big holly leaves on the front, it also has Christmas baubles all over the back, and when you press each of the baubles it plays a different festive tune. Can you believe that?

Ted looks at me like I'm nuts, of course, and comments that I moan constantly about having to wear the horrible green uniform to work, and how I'm not able to wear nice clothes, then as soon as I get the opportunity to wear nice clothes, I opt for a ridiculous Christmas jumper.

'But this is nice,' I say. 'I like it. It's fun and musical. Now I'm off, so don't delay me any longer, I need to get on the bus with all the animals for the manger.'

'Don't delay you? I was fast asleep and you woke me up.'

'Oh yes - sorry about that. Right, I'm going. See you later.'

I go to the kitchen and collect a large bin bag in which to transport all the stuffed animals I've got lined up in the hallway by the front door, ready to go into the nativity scene.'

Ted follows me, still rubbing his eyes like a giant toddler.

'Are these the animals for the nativity scene?' he says, as he watches me laying them carefully into a bin bag.

'Yes.'

'But they're ridiculous.'

'What's wrong with them? They'll make the nativity scene look wonderful.'

'An elephant, a camel and a horse? In the name of all that is holy, where do they fit in? There wasn't an elephant in the stable.'

'That's how the three wise men got to Bethlehem.'

'Yeah, on an elephant? Sure.'

'It's true. One was on an elephant; one was on a camel and the other was on a horse. I know I'm right because I went to the church and asked the vicar, just to be sure.'

'Was the vicar sober?'

I stand there, looking down at the bin bag, not keen to discuss this anymore because I'm just dying to get to work and get everything set up.

'Why are you in a sulk?' asks Ted.

'I'm not in a sulk, I just know how the three wise men got to Bethlehem and you don't, so keep your nose out of my elephant-related business.'

'OK,' he says, not quite sure whether I'm serious or joking.

I run out to the bus with my large bag of animals, struggle to get my mask on, and take a seat. I soon realise that I have to perch on the edge of the seat, because every time I sit back, my jumper touches the back of the seat and bursts into song. I didn't realise it was quite so sensitive. One little knock and there's a loud burst of music. I see people looking at their phones, wondering whether it's an incoming text that's causing the sudden musical outburst.

I'm about halfway through the journey when I burst into song without touching my jumper. It takes me a few minutes to realise that it's my phone, with a text from Ted.

'Can you get me some deodorant if you pass a shop? I'm stuck in the office all day and I'm desperate. I'm starting to smell like a horse, a camel and an elephant! xxx'

I get off the bus right next to Boots so I figure I'll get the deodorant straight away because I know I'll forget if I don't. I'll become so consumed with Christmas madness that all tasks and promises will be swept from my mind.

It's one of those really small branches of Boots that sells nothing but the absolute essentials. I walk in and head to where the deodorants are kept, but there only appear to be women's deodorants there. Do you think it matters? I mean - what difference can it really make? It must be all the same stuff inside, just with different patterns on.

But I know Ted won't be happy if I come back with a pink, floral deodorant bottle, so I ask the rather official looking woman behind the counter, wearing a white uniform, whether she has any men's deodorant.

'The ball kind?' she says.

Ball kind? What sort of bloody shop is this?

'No,' I screech. 'He just wants it for his underarms, thank you very much.'

. . .

When I arrive at Fosters Gardening and DIY centre, I head straight to Keith's office. Keith is the boss and a desk has been laid out for me in a corner of his office so I can manage all Christmas-related affairs.

It gives me such a sense of importance to have my own desk. I've been working at the centre since I left school, and I'm usually out in the store, avoiding customers and their questions, and whiling away time by moving plants about unnecessarily. But now I have a mission... I'm in charge of something. Christmas is all mine and I have a desk of my own on which to plan it.

I've made a start already, of course. Keith wanted me to hold back on the major attractions until today, but the Christmas decorations are already up. In retail we have the Christmas decorations up as soon as people stop wearing bikinis. Today, though, there is much more to behold: a big nativity scene, eight Christmas trees (including three madly decorated trees that I haven't told Keith about yet), a spectacular light display, and my *Christmas Post Box of Wishes and Dreams* in red and white, for people to post their Christmas wishes into.

I'm going to read the letters that they post and answer them from Santa's elf. We know it'll be mainly adults putting notes in there, because we don't get that many children in the store. All the same, I think it will be good fun.

I go and find Ray and Joe who have been seconded to help me with all the heavy lifting today. 'First let's get this nativity scene up and running,' I say, handing each of them a large box containing all manner of nativity features, the bag of animals I brought from home, a giant star, some hay and a makeshift stable.

I tried to use the stable I made last year, but someone had put spider plants on top of it and it was all dented and horrible, with worms crawling through it. It would have been very disrespectful to expect Mary and Joseph to live in a scruffy old stable like that, so I insisted on us commandeering the use of an enormous furniture packing box, big enough for me to get inside (I know that, because I did - to hide from Keith). I painted it and it looks bloody awesome.

The guys take the stable and all the contents over to where I have created an area for the nativity scene to live in what we've termed 'Christmas World' right next to Santa's grotto. There'll be music playing and sweets given out by elves, while Mary and Joseph sit in the middle of it all in all their magical festive splendour, flanked by the three wise men and the horse, camel and elephant on which they travelled.

Next, it's time to put up the Christmas trees, which I have decorated with my usual verve and individuality, by hanging pictures of Rick Astley stuck onto cardboard bells all over them. He lives locally and has promised to pop in and do a live song for us this Christmas so it seemed appropriate to have the trees decked out in his face. The other trees are slightly more sober, well – I say sober – one has little pink elephants hanging from every branch (don't dare ask me why there are elephants). The other tree has wildly different coloured ornaments hanging from every branch. I designed that to be a treat for everyone - a streak of wonder, colour and life.

It's a joyful scene and it really lifts the look of the store (and - be fair - it's quite a task to lift the look of a shop that sells mainly spades and copper piping).

The whole area is now a riot of colour, sound and joy. I commandeered a huge number of lights and we finish the whole scene off by stringing them above the whole area, like a sparkly net above it. The lights move from tree to tree, and to the edge of the portacabin and Santa's grotto, so you can see the section for miles off. To be fair, you can probably see it from Mars.

The only thing left to go up is the *Christmas Post Box of Wishes and Dreams* which I have lovingly created from numerous cereal boxes and an old Father Christmas outfit made from horrible scratchy nylon. The end result is spectacular. Well, it's certainly better than you might expect a bunch of cereal boxes and a nylon Father Christmas outfit to end up like.

I put a laminated note in front of the post-box saying '

Ho, ho, ho. I am the Christmas Post Box of Wishes and Dreams. Post your letters here with all your Christmas wishes, and I will see whether we can make them come true... from Santa's Elf.'

Keith warned me that writing that was asking for trouble.

'You don't know what guys are like,' he said, as if he were some worldly movie star who'd bedded most of the women in the universe, instead of the rather inefficient manager of a struggling DIY centre on the outskirts of Cobham.

He's a good boss, is Keith, but I'll be honest he's not the most sophisticated, and every so often he will say something so naff that I want to curl up and die.

'You'll be inundated with obscene requests and offensive suggestions,' he added when I first told him about the box. 'And that'll just be from me. Ha ha. Only joking. You know I'm joking, right? Mary. You know I'm joking?'

'Yes, Keith. I know you're joking.'

'Seriously though, I think it's a big mistake to call it

Christmas Post Box of Wishes and Dreams – just call it a Christmas Post Box. You're not going be making anyone's wishes and dreams come true. You're giving them false promises...false hope.'

I tried to argue that I was doing no such thing, and would be working very hard to 'make all their dreams come true. But Keith kept on about me changing the name of it, so in the end I said: 'Sure,' but I'm going to ignore him and call it what I want.

I'm just putting the finishing touches to the scene of wonderment and joy when Keith comes out to check on how I'm getting on. He stands with his hands in his pockets, staring at the scene.

'Wow,' he says. 'It's very bright. Very eye-catching. Very sparkly. That's a lot of lights.'

'Yes.'

'Why all the elephants?'

'That's how one of the three wise men got to Bethlehem.'

'On elephants? Do me a favour, Mary. They were on camels, everyone knows that.'

There are sniggers from Ray and Joe.

'One of them came on an elephant. I checked with a vicar.' My patience is already wearing thin with all the elephant defending, and I fear that this is only the beginning.

'How are you anyway, Ray. Family all good?'

'I'm OK,' says Ray.

'Well, cheer up then. You look bloody miserable. I thought your wife had left you or something.'

'Yeah well. She has. I told you before.'

Keith looks horrified. I've never seen anyone look so uncomfortable.

'Talk to Mary about it, Ray. Oh, and Mary - I've got some the staff together for a meeting at 4.30pm, can you come along and give them a quick overview of plans for Christmas, and what to expect.'

'Sure,' I say. I don't know what sort of plans he thinks I've got. I had a budget of £100 and was told to make a real splash. Most of that money went on pink elephants and lights.'

Still, at 4.30pm, I head to the meeting and walk to the front of the room, preparing to tell all my colleagues about the wonderful Christmas events we've got planned.

'Hello everyone, as you know my name is Mary Brown, and I'm in charge of Christmas,' I say, proudly. 'I want to run through some of the exciting things we've got planned for this year, and take any questions you might have. Also, if you have any questions relating to Christmas, or Christmas products, I'll be around to answer all your queries. So, let's get started....'

I run through all the glorious decorations that are now bedecking the walls, trees and plants, turning the DIY store into a spectacle of Christmas joy. There's not much reaction, to be honest. I hoped it would be a bit like one of those Trump rallies where everything you say is met by cheers and whoops of delight and waving of arms and chanting, but it doesn't really happen like that. They just sit there, mostly looking down, appearing to pay very little attention to what I'm saying as I bounce around in front of them, full of the joys of the season, squeezing the back of my jumper occasionally to inject some Christmas music and spirit into the occasion, and trying to make just one of them smile.

'OK, I'm glad that's all been received so well,' I say. 'Now I want to tell you about an exciting new development this year.

We are going to have a *Christmas Post Box of Wishes and Dreams*, so people can put their Christmas wishes into it, and Santa's elf will reply to them all.'

I look around the audience. Tony the Tap from bathroom supplies is playing with his phone, and Gavin from outdoor furniture is scratching his ears. I think that might be because he's got nits though. Gavin's always got some sort of horrible health condition, and we mostly keep away from him in case we catch it. Then I see his hand go up.

'Yes, Gavin?'

'How have you got an elf to answer the questions?'

'No, Gavin, it's not a real elf. That was just a joke.'

'Oh, so why are people going to post their Christmas wishes in the box?'

'It's just a bit of Christmas fun. And I'll be replying to them.'

'Will you be dressed as an elf?'

'Probably not. It doesn't make any difference, does it? It's just a bit of fun.'

Tony's hand goes up then.

'Do you have to have a stamp on the letter you put in the letterbox?'

'No, Tony. It's not a real letterbox.'

'What will you do if people put stamps on the letters?'

'I haven't really thought about that. Perhaps I will take them off the envelopes and give them to charity.'

'What charity?'

'Honestly, I haven't thought about that. I'll ask Keith what he thinks.'

'Do you think that the Mary and Joseph story is true?' asks Martina, the lady who works in the staff canteen.

'I really don't know,' I say. 'I'm not a history expert, and I don't have any religious studies background, they've just put me in charge of making the place look Christmassy.'

Keith interrupts and says we will leave it there, and he hopes everyone enjoys getting into the spirit of Christmas.

CHAPTER 2

STILL 15TH DECEMBER

'*I* need a drink,' I say to Belinda, as I slump into an armchair in the coffee room.

'There were some full-on, daft questions being asked there,' she says, sympathetically. 'Is it always like this?'

Belinda is new. She's the only woman working in the store who is around my age, everyone else is much older. I don't think she can believe how slow and behind the times some of them are.

'It's always like this,' I say.

She smiles.

'I think you're amazing. I mean - you're a sales assistant like me but you take on all this responsibility every Christmas. I would never be able to stand up and talk in front of everyone like that.'

'Thank you.'

'You should be in charge of this place. You seem so much brighter and more intelligent than everyone else.'

'Gosh, that would be nice. Especially the pay rise,' I say.

'Yeah.' She's playing with the rim of her plastic coffee cup as she sits there in silence...but it feels like she wants to ask me something, so I sit there in silence too, sipping my coffee.

'Can I ask you a question?' she says eventually. But then Tony the tap walks in and she looks up, all alarmed. She pulls her chair closer to mine.

'It's quite personal. Can I talk to you away from work? I don't know whether you fancy going for a drink tonight? I'm having a bit of an issue and I could do with talking through. There's a guy who is really coming on to me, and I'm finding it really awkward.'

'Sure,' I say. 'Who is it?'

She glances up at Tony.

'Do you mind if we talk about it later?' she mouths.

'No problem.'

There's a moment's silence.

'Could you give me a clue?'

'No,' says Belinda. 'Let's talk about it tonight. I don't want anyone to overhear. I've got my car, so I could drive us.'

'That would be great,' I say. Clearly I'm going to have to wait until tonight to hear who has been behaving inappropriately.

'Shall I meet you in the car park at 6? It's a blue golf.'

'See you then,' I say.

The rest of the day flies past. The staff don't seem to be wildly engaged with my Christmas festivities and some of them are walking around without their flashing Father Christmas hats on. To make it worse, they run away whenever they see me approaching clutching the hats that would be wearing. Happily, the customers seem to like what they see. They come wheeling through the store, then they stop and stare at the festive scene I've created, smiling up at the lights twinkling above them.

People laugh at the Christmas trees, and hover by the nativity scene, humming along to all the music. There's a genuine feeling of goodwill, and delight at the spiderweb of flashing, sparkling lights strung across the top of the nativity section.

By 6pm I'm feeling much better about everything. The team meeting put a dampener on things, but seeing the customers enjoying it has lifted my spirits. I've not seen anyone post a letter in my fabulous post box yet, but hopefully by the time I come in tomorrow morning there'll be a little bundle of them waiting for me.

Now I'm off to meet Belinda for a proper girly natter, and also – obviously – to find out which one of our employees has wandering hands. I've been thinking through the options since she first mentioned it. Keith can be a bit slimy, but I really don't think he's the handsy type. The guys in the warehouse are very loud and boisterous when they're all together, but they're pack animals, I can't imagine them causing any trouble when they're on their own, without backup. And they're quite sweet really. I can't see them causing any problems.

I walk out to the car park and see Belinda's car straight away...it's all shiny and new-looking, she must have bought it quite recently, or she keeps it looking nice. Funny - she doesn't strike me as the sort of woman who would spend a lot of time looking after her car. To be honest, she doesn't seem like the sort of woman who spends a lot of time looking after anything. I mean she seems really nice, but sort of scruffy and badly put together, if you know what I mean. I don't mean that as an insult at all, it's just that she's always scruffy.

As I walk over to her car, I see her coming out of the centre, so I drape myself across the bonnet to await her arrival. I assume a sort of amusing supermodel pose, lying perfectly still, with the poutiest of lips. I lay there for quite a while, thinking that Belinda should really be here by now. Perhaps she forgot something and had to rush back inside for it? When I look up, she's nowhere to be seen. I'll stay here a bit longer, but I'll turn on my other side for a bit because this is starting to get uncomfortable. I roll over, feeling the suspension groan beneath me as I do. And then I see it.

Bloody hell.

Sitting in the front of the car, looking ready to drive away are two people. I'm pouting and looking seductive, and they are just staring at me.

I jump off the bonnet, regretting the way it dips down as I leap to the ground, and hoping I haven't wrecked their suspension completely with my antics. Then I wave and run off. I don't know what else to do. I've no idea how to explain to them what I've just done.

I hear a car horn toot and turn round to see Belinda in a really scruffy old car. Much more like the sort of car I was expecting her to drive. The thing is practically falling apart. I jump into the passenger seat and instruct her to go.

'Who were they?' she asks, indicating the people sitting in the car on which I've just been lying. It's a fair enough question, I guess, but I don't have a sensible answer for her.

'Oh no one special. Just old friends,' I say. 'Quick, let's go.'

'I swear they were the guys who bought all that expensive garden furniture today. Your friends have good taste.'

'Yes,' I say, noncommittally.

'They're coming to collect it on Saturday before they move into their new house.'

'That's right. Yes - they're moving house. That's what I was just saying to them.'

'Oh right. Well, where shall we go for a drink?'

'King's Arms?'

Belinda pulls into the car park of the King's Arms and parks very badly, taking up two spots by parking on the dividing line between them, and then blocking another two by sticking her bumper out so far that she's effectively prevented anyone from getting into the spaces behind her. Four parking spots for one small car? That must be some sort of record.

We sit down in a corner booth and click our glasses of wine together.

'To Christmas,' says Belinda.

'Christmas,' I agree.

'I hope you didn't mind me asking you to come out tonight. I know you must be really busy with all your Christmas work,' says Belinda.

'Don't be silly,' I say. Really? How much work does she think it entails to string up some lights and make a post box out of cereal boxes?

'It's just so hard to know who you can talk about things to. You always seem so professional and so on top of things that I thought you might be able to help.'

This is not a common description of me, so I pause awhile to cherish the flattering words.

'I'm really happy to help,' I tell Belinda. 'Honestly, anything you tell me will be in confidence, and if there's anything I can do to assist or make life better at work, you only have to say.'

'No, this isn't at work,' says Belinda, and I regret that I feel a pang of disappointment.

'It's really embarrassing, but it's my mum's boyfriend. He keeps telling me how much he fancies me and I'm not sure what to do about it.'

'Oh right,' I say. 'That's a really difficult situation. Gosh. I'm sorry but I thought you meant one of the guys at work had been coming on to you, and I was going to suggest all sorts of things, but it's a bit harder if it's in your home.'

'Gosh, no. The guys at work are brilliant, they're so lovely and friendly I really like them. I think it's a great place to work. Keith's a bit weird though, isn't he?'

'Well yeah that's true. Weird but completely harmless,' I say.

'No, this is my mom's boyfriend. She's only been seeing him for a couple of months, and I don't like him at all. And he's now become a bit, you know, affectionate. Is that the right word? He strokes my hair when he walks past me, telling me how lovely I look.

'Mum smiles when he does it, she thinks it's great that we're all getting on. But we're not all getting on well at all. I'm certainly not getting on well with him. I'm sick to the back teeth of being touched by him.

'Then he got drunk last night and told me he really fancied me. I didn't know what to say.'

'Well, you tell him to piss off and you tell your mum straight way. Don't let someone in your own home make you feel scared and uncomfortable.'

'But I don't want to upset mum.'

'I promise you; your mum will be more upset if she thinks you've put up with horrible behaviour from him without telling her. She'll want to know. And she needs to know what sort of

17

scumbags she's going out with doesn't she? For her own good as well as yours.

'If you don't tell her you're not protecting her. You're leaving her vulnerable to more bad treatment from him, and you're making your own life very difficult.'

'Yeah, I guess,' says Belinda. 'I guess you're right. You know, I was thinking that maybe I should move out, or something like that. But that wouldn't be the right thing to do would it?'

'No, you've done nothing wrong. You need to tell your mum.'

'Yes, I'll tell her. I promise I'll talk to her. Thank you. I feel so much better now. I didn't want to move out and get a place of my own: I get so lonely. Do you live by yourself? I did it once and hated it.'

'Yes, I do, but my boyfriend Ted is around most of the time, so I never get lonely. I've also got this lovely friend called Juan who I met on a cruise years ago, and he's been living with me as well. Just as a friend, obviously. Ted wouldn't like it if I moved another boyfriend in.'

Belinda laughs and looks at me with admiration.

'I'd love to have a boyfriend,' she says. 'It must be amazing. Just having someone there who loves you, no matter what. And you can tell them anything. And everything's lovely. Just this gorgeous perfect man at home waiting for you.'

I get the sentiments of what she's saying. But when I think of Ted scratching his balls and picking his nose, the words 'perfect man' don't spring easily to mind.

'How did you meet Ted? I don't know how to meet anyone. I've never really had a boyfriend.'

'I met Ted at this club I went to.' I don't want to tell her that we met at Fat Club, so I tail off before explaining what sort of club, and offer her advice instead.

'I think your best bet is to get out as much as you can. You are never going to meet someone in your house, so you need to get out, join clubs, even go to the gym if you can bear it. I know it's one of the most dreadful places on earth, but it is full of men. Or even go to a cafe and sit and drink a coffee and look around. You know there are lots of places you can go where you might meet someone. And have you tried internet dating?'

'No, I could never do that.' says Belinda. 'Honestly, I'd hate it.'

I certainly don't feel like advocating for her to join an internet dating site. I went on one once, when Ted and I stopped seeing one another for a few months. It was the most surreal experience of my life. So, I just smile at her, and say that I understand.

'The first thing you need to do is go home and talk to your mum.'

'I will,' she promises. 'Mum and her boyfriend are away this week. They are back on Sunday, and I'll talk to her then.'

'And you'll tell her how upset this is all making you?'

'I will,' she promises, and we clink our glasses together once again.

CHAPTER 3

16TH DECEMBER

*O*K, my first task on this lovely, though chilly, morning is to head out to the grotto and make sure all the sparkly lights and music are on. I'd originally thought of playing carols through the music system, but I'll be honest with you - I noticed last year that there wasn't a lot of interest in the Christmas area when we had 'Away in a Manger' filtering out through the second-rate music system, but when I switched it over to a mixture of Christmas favourites, the punters rolled in. I even saw a few of them sing along to *Last Christmas*. It might not say much for the sophistication and religiosity of the good folk of Cobham, but they definitely prefer Wham to choir boys, so that's what I'm giving them.

Once I'm happy that the place looks utterly adorable, I turn my attention to the *Christmas Post Box of Wishes and Dreams*, sitting proudly before me. I open the little door that I fashioned on the front of it and stick my hand inside.

Oh my God.

There are letters in there. I feel a thrill rush up through my body. I mean - I *hoped* there would be letters, but there actually *are* letters. I count them. There are 12 in total. Oh my God. I pull them out, tie the whole thing back down again, and disappear into the office to read them and pen answers. I'm quite good at giving advice and offering kind words, I just hope I can help with these.

I sit down at my desk and open the first one. I swear to God - some people are rude. I mean - really rude. I'm not even sure whether I should tell you what they wrote, but very many of the suggestions would not be anatomically possible. And the suggestions about the reindeers' antlers? Who thinks like that?

I put the rude letters to one side and discover, to my great disappointment, that there are only three left that aren't obscene.

The first of these says: 'I wish the store was cheaper.' and the second says: 'I wish someone in this place knew the difference between a flat top grind saw and a triple chip grinder.'

I can't do anything about the prices in the store, but I plan to send a formal letter back to the writer of the second letter, explaining that there are lots of people here who can help with particular tools, and giving him the name of a member of staff who he can contact.

I expected to busy all morning, writing letters and trying to find the answers to problems, I feel a wave of disappointment that I won't be able to help people in the way I thought I would.

As I sit pondering the situation, and feeling annoyed that Keith was right - there were lots of obscene letters in the post box, I can hear the sounds of frying coming from the canteen with sits next to Keith's office. As soon as I hear frying, I think of chips. And now that I've got chips on my mind, I'm distracted beyond belief. I feel thrown off course, as my mind drifts off to consider the glorious smell of vinegar on hot chips. That moment when you walk away from the chip shop and tear through the grease and vinegar-softened paper to reveal gorgeous honey-brown chips beneath, like rays of potato sunshine. Oh God.

I find myself googling where the nearest chippy is, and wondering whether I can get out there and buy a packet. It's too early. Nowhere will be open at 10am in the morning, but my mouth doesn't seem to understand that, as it salivates madly. All I can think about is the thought of ripping the paper and feeling the warmth of the chip-scented steam rise up. The tangy and delicious combination of salt and vinegar sprinkled and splashed across the lovely fat wodges of deliciousness.

This is one of the things I find most difficult about having this food obsession. I'm quite happy, going along, doing something utterly unrelated to food then suddenly a word, smell or sound will remind me of food and I'm off into a trance and thinking about food. Now I can't stop thinking about chips.

Are you like that?

It's not so much that I'm greedy, or can't stop eating when I'm in front of food (though I confess that I do that too!), it's deeper than that. It's like I have a bell in my head that rings every time anything that could be even remotely linked to food or eating is mentioned. It forces me to start obsessing about food even though I'm not hungry, and my obsession isn't just with thinking, my thoughts become so real and so vivid that I feel driven to act. I don't want chips because I'm hungry, I want them because something has triggered the thought in my mind and now the compulsion to act on that thought has overwhelmed me.

It's a bit like that Pavlov's Dog experiment. Have you heard of that? A scientist called Ivan Pavlov found that objects, sights, sounds and smells could trigger a conditioned response that was nothing to do with the original trigger. In his experiment he rang a bell every time he fed his dogs, so the animals made a mental link between the sound of the bell and food. From then on, every time he rang the bell, the dogs would salivate.

The experiment was a breakthrough because we associate salivation with hunger, but in this case it wasn't. The dogs weren't hungry, they salivated when they heard a bell. Their response was down to their psychology rather than biology.

So - that's the science and psychology lecture over. I mention it because I feel a bit like that...as if all sorts of things, all the time, trigger a reaction in me and I need to eat. Not because I'm hungry or greedy, but for some other reason, and I don't know what it is.

'You look miles away,' says Keith, coming into the office to see me. 'What on earth are you thinking about?'

'Dogs and bells and lovely chips.'

'Not more mad things to go in the manger with the elephants, I hope.'

I decline the chance to tell him about the wise man who travelled on an elephant, and go back to the letters in my hand. Keith's arrival has broken the instant, all-consuming intensity of the desire to buy chips, and now the thought sits in my mind like a small but terrifying dog. And I know whilst the thought might seem cuddly and harmless, if anyone mentions chips, or anything happens to upset me emotionally, the dog will bark furiously and I'll be down to Super Cod before you can say 'battered sausage.' But for now, I'm OK, the anxiety has eased and I can get on with my day.

So, it's back to the letters. Or one letter, more accurately. Underneath the pile of loosely folded letters is a letter in an envelope with neat handwriting on the outside. The envelope is pale blue and the writing neatly slanted and elegant...as if written by a quill-wielding, sophisticated gentleman from the early 1900s.

Inside the envelope is a letter: not written on matching pale blue paper, which is disappointing, but on plain white A4 paper. It's typed so clearly hasn't come from the early 1900s, another great disappointment.

Daniel.Johnson@gmail.com

Dear Father Christmas,

I wish I had a girlfriend for Christmas. I feel so lonely sometimes.
   Can you help arrange a date for me?
   I am free on 20th December if that would be possible.

Kind regards,

Daniel

I turn over the page but there's nothing written on the back. No address, no phone number. Gosh. It's a sweet little note, and I feel a rush of desire to help, but I'm not sure how to do that. I suppose I could put up a note in the centre asking all single women to nominate themselves for a date. Perhaps I could run a competition…

Win a date with Mr Lonely from Surrey?

Na. There's no way Keith would let me do that. Not in a million years. But there must be something I can do.

I pull out of the envelope again and look at the writing. I have such a lovely feeling about this guy. I've no idea how old he is, of course. He could be in his 50s or 60s for all I know, but I see him being a couple of years older than me, romantic beyond his years, chivalrous and kind. As I'm pondering the situation, Bev from key cutting and electricals walks past, and pulls a face at me through the window. I pull an equally silly face back before Belinda walks along and pulls a daft face at me. I pull another silly face back. We always do this. Instead of greeting one another like adults, we've taken to gurning at each other. It's most peculiar.

Hang on.

Belinda is really keen to meet someone.

Daniel and Belinda.

That would be perfect.

'Belinda,' I say, rushing out of the office, clutching the letter in my hand. I catch up with Belinda who has caught up with Bev, and they both stop and turn round as I charge towards them with all the grace of a stampeding rhinoceros.

'Look,' I say, brandishing the letter at Belinda. 'Read this letter.'

Belinda reads it and looks up at me. 'Wow. He sounds nice. But what does he look like?' she asks.

'Well, that's the problem. I've no idea.'

'Is he my age?'

'I don't know that either. It's just come...it was put in the *Christmas Post Box of Wishes and Dreams*. Do you want me to investigate further?'

'Does he live nearby?'

'I guess so,' I say. 'I mean, he must leave fairly nearby or he wouldn't come to this centre. And look how neat it all is. He must have seen the post box going up yesterday, gone home to write a letter, then come back to post it. So I imagine he lives near. If I can find out, would you like to go on a date with him?'

'Er...yes,' she says. 'I mean - yeah, why not. Just make sure he's not, like, 60 or something though.'

'Yes, of course,' I say. 'So - you're sure? I can go ahead and plan it.'

'Yeah - what the hell. It's Christmas, and I've had a shit year. Go for it, girl, and let me know where we're going.'

'Great. I'll contact him now.'

'Just make sure he's not too old,' shouts Belinda as I walk away. 'I'm 23, I don't want to date my Grandfather.'

'I will. Are you free on Saturday?'

'I am at lunchtime,' she says.

'OK, I'll try and arrange something for Saturday lunchtime.'

I get back to the office and wonder exactly what I should do to 'make sure he's not too old.' I'll have to email him. It's going to be a pretty embarrassing email, but it has to be done, so here I go:

Dear Daniel,

. . .

Thank you so much for your letter in the Christmas Wishes Post-box. I'm sorry to hear that you feel lonely. We'd love to set up a lunch date for you, with a lovely girl, here in the DIY centre on Saturday 20th at 1pm. Do you have a picture that you could send us? Also, I hope you don't mind me asking this, but are you under 40?

Thanks very much Mary 'Christmas' Brown.

It's just minutes before a reply is forthcoming.

'Thank you. Yes, I'm under 40 and I would love to go on a date.'

No photo, but as long as he's under 40, that'll be fine. Belinda's lovely, but she's not going to win Miss World anytime soon. I know that sounds cruel, but all I'm saying is that looks aren't everything, and if he's in the right ballpark, age-wise, I think we should give it a go.

I send an email to Belinda confirming that the date is on Saturday, and I send a quick email to Keith to tell him about it, then I settle down to think of some PR ideas, some ways in which we can get the press down to spread the story of Christmas romance. If there's a strong PR or marketing opportunity through it, then Keith will say yes to the date, if there isn't, he won't be interested.

CHAPTER 4

STILL 16TH DECEMBER

*B*y the time Keith comes back from lunch I've created a multi-dimensional PR campaign that would rival that of any political strategist. Except that, unlike the Brexit campaigners, I haven't written things on the side of a bus. No - I've just put together bits of A4 paper and Post It notes. But don't let the unsophisticated look of the thing detract from its power. This is designed to impress.

'What the hell's that?' asks Keith, unravelling himself from scarves, hat, gloves and thick winter coat, and peering at my life's work as if it's something I've picked out of the bin.

'It's a PR campaign to tell the world about the great Christmas stuff we've got going on here at the store.'

'What great Christmas stuff? You've put up some lights, Mary, and they look great, but it's not exactly Lapland. I don't think the press will be interested.'

'I've done more than just lights. There are loads of things going on.' I feel wounded. Has he not been out there? 'There's the letterbox to send wishes to Santa who will answer all of them - except the really rude ones. And there's the grotto and all the trees with wonderful decorations. And there's the nativity scene'

'A nativity scene with a bloody elephant in the middle of it.'

He throws his hat and scarf onto the hat stand and they miss the pegs, slide down the coats and land on the floor. He shakes his head as if it's the fault of the hat and scarf, and stomps over to pick them up.

'I'm not criticising anything, Mary. I gave you a tiny budget and you've done a sterling job. All I'm saying is that I don't think it's a story that the global media will be interested in.'

'Yes, but the date will be.'

'What date?'

'Did you not see the email I sent you?'

'No Mary, I haven't seen anything. I've been out with my wife trying to pick carpets and I actually don't care at all what carpets we have. And now I've wasted my entire lunch break comparing duck egg blue Axminster carpets with seafoam coloured Wiltons and I'm fed up.'

I pause for a moment while Simona brings him his coffee which she puts onto the edge of his desk. Keith then swings his legs onto the desk and I swear to God I think he's going to kick the scalding coffee all over her. We both gasp.

'I know what I am doing,' he says. 'My feet weren't anywhere near the coffee cup. Now, tell me about this date. What's that about?'

'OK,' I say. 'Well, a lonely man put a note into the *Christmas Post Box of Wishes and Dreams* to say that he'd love to meet someone this Christmas. It was a sweet note in which he said he gets lonely sometimes, so I thought it would be a great idea if we fixed him up with someone.'

'And who, pray, are we planning to fix him up with?'

'A member of staff who is single and keen to meet someone. She's lovely and she's lonely too. I was going to organise a date to fix them up. A date here in the centre, in the grotto. A Christmas love story. On Saturday.'

'Oh. That sound doesn't sound like a bad idea, Mary. Who's the female on the staff?'

'It's Belinda.'

'Oh.'

There's a short silence while I wait for him to say more than 'Oh,' but he doesn't, so I carry on.

'I think it could be a lovely story. It will bring attention to the Post Box of Christmas Wishes and Dreams, and all we're doing at the centre to make Christmas as special as possible for the community.'

'Yes, that's wonderful. I love it. I'm just wondering about Belinda as the date. Do we not have anyone a bit - you know - more attractive? A bit thinner?'

There. He said it.

'Belinda's lovely,' I say.

'Yes, I've no doubt. I'm just thinking about the photographs and the reputation of the centre.'

'What?'

'Oh, it doesn't matter. I just think that if possible, we should get someone pretty. Someone photogenic. How about Selina? She's a lovely attractive girl.'

'Yes, she's also engaged. Belinda is perfect.'

I can see Keith is still thinking, casting his mind through all the more attractive women on the staff.

'I'll get on with setting it up then. I thought we'd do it here in the centre. We can decorate the pagoda with the flowers from the cut stems department and bring out the lovely gardening furniture and make it gorgeous, but also a big advert for everything we sell in the store.'

'Oh, that does sound like a good idea. Very well - you plan it all and keep me briefed. Is Mandy single? She's a nice-looking girl.'

'I don't know, but Belinda is and she's keen to go on this date.'

'Very good,' says Keith, picking up his phone. 'Just make sure we look good. Oh, and stop calling it the *Christmas Post Box of Wishes and Dreams*. It's just a Christmas Post Box.'

I'm due to finish work at 3pm because I was in at 7am this morning, so I need to get cracking and work out how we're going to organise this date. Mum's coming in after work to take me Christmas shopping which I'm really looking forward to, but it means I have to leave on time, no staying late to get things done.

I open a new word document on my computer... OK, so - what are the issues.

I know that Keith will baulk at us spending too much money on this date, so we'll have to get a nice take away or something for them to eat. There's a lovely Lebanese restaurant in Hampton Court, I'll email them now. Perhaps they will give us a discount if I tell them about the publicity.

The decor should be easy enough to do, since we're in a store full of lovely gardening furniture and flowers. I wonder whether we could get a snow machine? We could have people dressed as angels and snowflakes all around so the whole thing is white and sparkling and beautiful. I jot all this down. Next, I send out press releases, inviting local journalists to meet the lucky shopper who is invited on a magical Christmas date.

This is going to be perfect. Just perfect.

CHAPTER 5

STILL 16TH DECEMBER

I see mum wandering through the garden centre at around 2.30pm, she's dressed nicely, but clutching a carrier bag. What is it with mums and carrier bags? I've lost count of the number of handbags I've given to her as presents over the years, but she still brings a carrier bag because she wants to keep the handbags for best.

I don't know what 'best' is though. It seems to be a term used by people born just after the war when things were tight and they got used to only ever having one of anything, and having to keep it in the best nick possible. I keep telling her that she should use the bags I buy her and if they get lost or damaged, I'll just buy her new ones. But she won't have it.

'This bag's just fine,' she says, indicating the aged Sainsbury's carrier bag she has wrapped around her wrist.'

'I want you to have nice things and use them,' I tell her. 'There's no point having them if you don't use them.'

'OK, I promise I will,' she says.

'Now come and see the decorations.' I give her a hug and lead her in the direction of the nativity scene.

I have to say that she's impressed with what she sees. 'You have done very well there, dear. The way you have done those lights is wonderful. And the trees with all those amazing decorations! You do have a magical way with colour.'

This is another thing about mums. They can be desperately nice about you even when you've created what is, to all other eyes, a complete eyesore.

'Thanks very much,' I say. 'What do you think of the nativity scene. Don't you love the way the children are sitting around looking at it.'

'Yes yes,' says mum. Then she goes quiet.

'What's the matter? Didn't you think it was great?'

'You know that I think everything you do is great,'

'But...'

'Oh Mary, you know I don't like to criticise, but I suppose I was a bit surprised to see an elephant in there. I've never read a bible story in which there is an elephant in the manger.'

'Not you as well.'

'What do you mean?'

'Everybody is telling me that there was no elephant there. But you look back at the Bible. The three wisemen arrived on an elephant, a camel and a horse. That's how they got there.'

'Well, every Christmas card I've seen, and every nativity I've watched, the wisemen come on camels. It's that part of the world, isn't it? The part of the world with camels.'

'Yes, but one of them definitely comes on an elephant. You flick through your bible when you get home and check.'

'I will,' she says.

We leave the centre and catch the bus to Richmond where we wander through the shops, picking up bits and pieces for presents. I find a giant chocolate 'T' covered in marzipan, with nuts sprinkled on the top, to put into Ted's stocking. Then I pick a second one up because I know that there is no way on God's good earth, that I will make it to Christmas without nibbling on it.

'You should get one for dad,' I say. 'He loves marzipan, doesn't he? He always picks it off the top of the Christmas cake which really annoys everyone.'

'Oh Mary, that's a very good idea. You're right. He does absolutely adore marzipan.'

She picks up the T.

'But dad's name doesn't begin with T? Why would you pick up a T?'

'I don't know. Why did you pick up the letter T?'

'Because Ted's name begins with T.'

'Oh yes, I see what you mean.'

She eventually buys a collection of letters for people she knows, and I'm delighted to report that she gets the right letter for the right name. What an earth would she do if I weren't here?

I pick up some lovely earrings for the girls, in Zara, and some other bits and pieces like a hot water bottle in the shape of a zebra and a pair of gloves that squeal when you clap your hands. Honestly, it must be absolutely great being one of my friends at Christmas. Who wouldn't want to wake up to a pair of gloves, squealing under the tree?

'Come on. Let's go and have a drink. It is nearly Christmas after all.'

'Sure,' I say, because - who'd say no to a cheeky afternoon

drink? But it's most unusual of mum to suggest alcohol at all, let alone before 6pm.

We wander into a bar that is absolutely packed with Christmas revellers, many of them sporting their finest Christmas jumpers. In the corner there's a group of people sitting down to a proper Christmas meal. At a guess I'd say it was a work party, and the people there seem to be at various levels of drunkenness. There is definitely a relationship between how drunk they seem and how much fun they are having. The sober-looking guys glance at their watches and wonder when they can get back to the office and away from all the forced jollity, while their more inebriated workmates throw tinsel at one another and smile an awful lot.

'What do you fancy to drink?' I ask mum.

'Whatever you're having, love,' she says.

'No. You choose what you want. Don't just have what I'm having.'

'I don't know. Your father gets me a glass of wine, but I'm not that keen on wine, to be honest.'

'What do you like?'

'I like ginger wine but it makes my cheeks go bright red... ginger always does that to me. I enjoy it though.'

'OK, go and sit down and I'll get you a ginger wine.'

The barman pours the glass of Stones ginger wine and it's such a tiny amount, that I tell him to make it a double, and decide to have one myself.

Mum has sat herself down on a long table next to a rather drunk-looking man with three pints in front of him. I have to be honest - it's the last place I would have sat. I'd rather be next to the festive-jumper clad work group, or the old guys sitting at the bar with no tinsel or decoration of any kind. But a man sitting on his own at lunchtime with three pints in front of him? He's going to start talking to us, isn't he?

I sit down next to mum, and put her glass in front of her, moving my eyes towards the old guy in the coat, as if to say to her: 'why are you sitting next to him?'

'I thought he might be lonely,' she mouths back at me. Bless her. We can't even come for a Christmas drink without her trying to help someone out.

I smile over at the man.

'You're wondering why on earth I have three pints in front of me, aren't you?'

'I thought you were probably just thirsty,' says mum, taking a large gulp of her ginger wine. Her cheeks turn bright pink straight away. It's amusing to watch.

The man, meanwhile, takes a sip of one pint, then the other pint, then the third pint.

'I bet you are wondering why I'm drinking them like this, aren't you?'

'Not at all,' I reply. I'm not wildly interested in anything he does, but he seems desperate to talk to me and explain his situation.

'I have three brothers. One brother lives in Australia, one in China, and one in the States. We can't be together this Christmas, and it's the first Christmas since our parents died that we've not been able to get together,' he says.

'I'm sorry to hear that.' I take a large gulp of my ginger wine and feel my cheeks flush.

'Oooo - it's happened to you too,' says mum, with a giggle. 'Your cheeks have gone pink.'

I touch my cheeks lightly as our new friend continues with his story.

'We made a vow to each other that at Christmas all four of us would go to bars in our respective countries and drink together. So right now, my brothers have four Guinness Stouts too, and we're drinking together - all four brothers.'

'I can't help but notice that you only have three pints in front of you, but you said there were four of you.'

'Yes, but I'm not having one...I've given up drinking,' he says. There's a pause of a few minutes before he collapses with laughter, banging his hands on the table and creasing over with mirth.

The guys at the bar laugh too. 'You've given up drinking so you only have three pints. It works every time,' they howl.

'Come on, drink up,' I say to mum. 'We're getting out of here.'

The man continues to laugh to himself, raising a glass as we leave the pub.

'Do you think that man has sat in the pub all day like that, with three pints in front of him, ready to crack that joke?' I say to mum. 'Because if he has, he's having a very dull Christmas.'

'You know, I think he probably has, the daft fool.

We leave the pub and mum looks down the busy street. 'I'm going to head back. I've left your father on his own for too long. You know what he's like if I leave him. He'll start putting on old John Wayne films. He needs me there to keep him in order.'

'No, don't go home yet, come with me. Dad will be OK. If the worse thing he's going to do is watch old cowboy films, I'm sure he'll be fine for another couple of hours.'

'I suppose so,' says mum. 'What shall we do then? Look for another pub?'

'Have you got a problem or something? Shall I find you an AA meeting?'

'No, but that ginger wine was nice, wasn't it? I must remember to get us a bottle for Christmas.'

'Good thinking,' I say. 'It does give us both very pink cheeks though. If we drink too much more we'll look like beetroots.'

'Look there's a bench here, let's sit down while we work out what to do.'

I forget that mum's getting older. It wouldn't have occurred to me to sit down, but when you're over 60, I guess you get tired. Mum and I went to a health farm a few years ago. Actually - no - it wasn't a health farm at all - it was a military training camp. We *thought* we were going to a health farm. Bloody hell. It nearly killed me. Any way, the reason I mention it is because Mum was up and exercising several times a day, and seemed really fit and healthy. Even in the two years since then, I've noticed her ageing. I can't stand the thought of mum and dad getting old.

I sit on the bench next to mum, and smile at her. 'Shall we find somewhere a bit nicer than a pub? How about we find somewhere where we can get afternoon tea and ginger wine?'

'Oh, that would be lovely, dear. But where?'

'I guess one of the hotels will do afternoon tea. Let me check.'

I google the hotels in Richmond and discover that the Hill Crest hotel, about five minutes from where we're sitting, does them.

'I've found somewhere,' I say to mum, but she's completely distracted by a runner approaching us. I look more closely and see that he's naked.

'Mum! He's not wearing any clothes!' I say, while my mother stares.

He passes us - his bits and pieces bobbing and swaying as he goes.

'Blimey, I almost had a stroke,' said mum.

'Me too, mum, but I couldn't quite reach,' I joke back.

'No - a stroke. You know - when you collapse and your face goes funny.'

'Yes, I know, I'm only joking with you. Come on. We need sandwiches and cakes.'

We walk up the hill to the hotel. Google lied to me. It's a good half hour walk, and I am carrying all the bags because I am worried about mum being old and not wanting her to get any older. Finally, the beautiful old hotel hovers into view.

'I bet this will be lovely,' I say.

'I bet it will, love,' says mum.

CHAPTER 6

17TH DECEMBER

By the time Keith makes it into the office the next morning, I'm a wreck. I'm lying across my desk sobbing uncontrollably. I just can't stop.

'Good lord, woman, what an earth is wrong with you?' he says, displaying all the sensitivity and kindness that I've come to expect from him. He's not a man to deal gently with emotional outbursts. To him, every moment of emotion is weakness and needs to be stamped out at all costs.

'It's one of the letters,' I say to him, gasping between sobs and trying to get the words out. 'A young boy. He's only five, and his dad has put a letter in the *Christmas Postbox of Wishes and Dreams* saying how much he wants to go to Lapland. He was born with one leg and has this horrible illness that might end up killing him in the next few years, and there is a photo, and he's gorgeous.

'He is lovely. Look at him. We have to send him to Lapland.

Somehow, we have to be able to get this kid and his family to go to Lapland. Look, Keith. Look at him...'

I thrust the picture of the beautiful blonde kid in front of Keith. The child has wide blue eyes and a soft gentle smile. He looks from the picture like any other five-year-old boy, and without reading the letter I would just have thought he was a fun-loving kid with lots of friends. But now I realise his life has been misery. And the only thing he wants is a trip to Lapland.

Keith looks at the picture and grudgingly admits that it's all rather sad, before saying: 'That's life, girl. I'm afraid there's a lot of shit around.'

'I know, I realise that. But we have the opportunity to help one child, and make life just a little bit less shit for him and his family. Can the company pay for him to go? It would be such an amazing PR opportunity.'

'Yeah right, it's been so tight this year they won't pay for anything, let alone thousands of pounds to send a kid to Lapland. Do you know how much of a struggle it was for me to get the bathroom section painted? And that only set them back £100, and the paint was from the store. I had to fill in 45 forms for that.'

'Can we try? Please let me contact them and explain how wonderful this would be for us.'

'No, Mary. Absolutely not. If you want to send me an email with the details, and all the likely costings, I'll send it through to head office, but I think the chances of someone from head office being willing to foot the bill are about as likely as the chances that one of the three wise men came to Bethlehem on the back of a bloody elephant.'

'Well then, there's every chance they'll say yes, because there is no doubt in my mind that one of the three wise men did come to Bethlehem on an elephant. Why does everyone doubt me?'

'Because it's a nutty suggestion. Put an email together and I'll do my best, but the chances are about 1% of you getting any money out of headquarters. And don't go separately contacting them yourself. Do you understand?'

'I understand,' I say, but I know, in that moment, somehow, I have to get that child on a trip to Lapland with his parents.

I switch on my computer to find out how much the trip will cost.

Ideally, we'd go, say, 22nd December, back on the 24th December. I realise that will be the most expensive time of year to go to Lapland.

I look down through the figures.

Blimey.

I wasn't expecting it to be cheap, but I'm shocked by the cost. The company simply aren't going to go for this. I go back into the search engine and suggest going on the 23rd, just staying one night and coming back on the 24th. It's marginally cheaper, of course, but still recklessly expensive. The best part of £5k. Shit. Keith is never going to go for this.

Still, I can only try. I put an email together with all the figures on it, and a summary of why this would be such a lovely thing to do, and also a valuable thing in terms of the promotion that the shop would get, and I email it over to him. I attach a picture of the child, then I sit back with my fingers crossed hoping, with every fibre of my being, that this trip can go ahead.

Dear Keith,

. . .

As you are aware, we had a very lovely letter appearing in the Christmas Post Box of Wishes and Dreams this morning, from the father of a young boy called Oliver. Oliver was born with a degenerative disease, and with only one leg.

He is a happy, friendly boy who absolutely loves Christmas, and the father's wish was for them to be able to take little Oliver to Lapland.

I wondered whether the company would be willing to fund the trip, because it would attract lots of positive publicity for us, and show how kind and loving we are as a company, and keen to invest in all the community around us.

I have to confess that the trip would not be cheap. I've looked at the most cost-effective way of doing it, and it would still cost around £5000 to get their family of three to Lapland for a couple of days. I do appreciate how expensive this is, and how tight things are across the entire retail industry, but I think that we would be more than compensated for by the incredible goodwill that would be generated in the local community, and the great publicity that our kindness would bring.

If you need any more information, please do contact me.

Just to repeat, even though it is an expensive trip, it's my belief that we would have lots of marketing and PR opportunities as a result of it, and it would work out to be worth doing.

Kind regards,

Mary 'Christmas' Brown

It doesn't take long before Keith replies.

. . .

Mary, that's just not going to happen. Is there no cheaper trip? Can we not send them to a Christmassy hotel down the road or something? Or send them one of the hampers from the seasonal goods section? If it's more than a few hundred quid, there's no point me even emailing Head Office. Keith

PS Don't call it the Christmas Post Box of Wishes and Dreams

I reply back in email, even though he's sitting a few metres from me.

But Keith, it's Lapland, it's bound to be expensive. My point is that it would be worth it. Pleeeeeease try. Please!

Keith leaves the office without acknowledging my reply to him, and I see him stroll through the centre, passed my nativity scene where there's an elephant that absolutely SHOULD be in there, and off to hardware, presumably to have a sneaky fag by the exit next to the nails. He thinks we don't know, but the horrible mixture of stale smoke and mints when he comes back gives away both the fact that he has been smoking and that he's trying to hide it.

'There aren't huge crowds here,' he says on his return. 'Don't these people know it's almost Christmas? Mary, think of some ways in which we can pull people in. You know - like last year when the place was overrun with shoppers.'

'If we sent the little boy to Lapland, we'd get great publicity and people would hear about the good work we do, and they'd come here for sure,' I try, but the response is predictable.

'OK Mary. Let me rephrase that...how do we get lots of good publicity without spending five grand that the company doesn't have?'

'We've got the MCD on Saturday - there's interest in that. Two local papers, Surrey Life magazine and Women Online. They're coming. I'm sure it will show us in a great light, and part of helping the community and draw people in.'

'What on earth is MCD? I thought you were running everything past me.'

'The Magical Christmas Date. I did run it past you.'

'Oh that. Yes, of course you did. Well, that's good. I look forward to that. When is it again?'

'On Saturday. I'll send another press release out in the morning and see whether I can get any more interest.'

'Good, good. Well, I'll leave you to it then. And I will send off that letter you wrote to headquarters. Just in case someone there is feeling very generous, or full of the Christmas spirit...or drunk, or something. Just don't hold out any hope of it getting anywhere.'

'I'll call Oliver's dad back and tell him that we're seeing what we can do,' I say.

'No, Mary. Don't do that, for God's sake. Just leave it until head office comes back. Don't make any promises to him.'

'Sure,' I say, but I feel so sad about it all. That little boy's picture keeps haunting me...fancy being born with just one leg? I need to get out of the office before I burst into tears, so I head out past the nativity scene and to the bench on the far side of the centre, where I often slip off to, to while away the hours.

Today I can't stop thinking about Oliver.

I pull the letter out of my pocket and read through it once more. The words make me want to cry all over again. Before I can think straight, I have rung the number on the letter. I just want to tell the father that I have the letter, and reassure him that I'll do all I can. I want to tell him that it's difficult, and I'm not promising anything, but I'll do everything possible.

'Is that Oliver's father?' I say to the softly-spoken man who answers the phone.

He mumbles that it is and requests that tell him who I am.

I go through a lengthy explanation of how I'm in charge of Christmas. I hear him sigh.

'No, I'm not pretending to be in charge of Christmas round the world. I'm not claiming to be Father Christmas or anything. I'm not a nutter. I promise. I just received your letter about Oliver. I'm from Foster's Gardening & DIY centre.'

'Oh, I see. Oh yes. Right,' says Oliver's dad, sounding mightily relieved. 'I thought you were one of those people pretending to be a charity campaigner, but just trying to get money out of me.'

'Gosh no, no. Not at all.'

'You've caught me at a bit of a bad time, actually. I'm in hospital in Scotland with Ollie.'

'Oh sorry,' I say.

'Yes, things haven't been great recently. It's three years today since my wife died - Ollie's mum - and Ollie's not well at all.'

Oh My God. His wife died.

'I just wanted to say that we will arrange a trip to Lapland for you and your son to go on. It would be our pleasure. I can email you later with all the details.'

'You're joking?'

'No, I'm being serious.'

'Oh, that's wonderful. Absolutely wonderful. Thank you so much. That will make Ollie's day. He'll be so pleased. Thank you from the bottom of both of our hearts. My name's Brian, by the way.'

'Great, well I hope that cheers Ollie up.'

'It will. He'll be delighted. Oh that's great. I didn't know whether a store would have the budget to do charity trips like this.'

'Of course, yes, the management at Fosters are very keen on helping people.'

'Well thanks again. Thank you. I can't tell you how much this means.'

'You're very welcome,' I say, before ending the call and staring off into the middle distance. What have I done? I mean - what in God's name have I done?

I need to call Juan. He'll know what to do.

'Ciao,' he says, breezily.

'Oh God, Juan. I've just done something completely insane. I've got myself into a mess. I've promised this lovely man something that I can't deliver and I don't know quite what to do.'

'Oooo...what have you been promising strange men?'

'I promised him that he and his one-legged son could have a free trip to Lapland.'

CHAPTER 7

STILL 17TH DECEMBER

I hear Juan giggle on the end of the line.

'No, this is not funny. This is weapons grade stupid,' I say to him. 'I'm not joking, it's not the first line of a clever joke. I have behaved in a way that is properly God Damned stupid.'

'Explain,' he says.

I hear the clink of glass. 'Are you drinking already?'

'Yes, just a little one, my lovely friend. Tell me what's going on.'

I regal Juan with the story of the *Christmas Post Box of Wishes and Dreams* and the letter and then my call to the little boy's dad.

'What's wrong with that?' says Juan. 'It sounds like you've behaved perfectly properly.'

'No, Juan. I accidentally promised him a free trip to Lapland but there is no free trip to Lapland. I made it up. Now I need to provide a free trip.'

I hear spluttering and a small cry of anguish down the phone.

'You made me choke,' he says. 'That's the craziest thing ever. Why would you do that? Why? I mean - what are you going to do? He has a disabled son...you can't let him down. You have to provide a trip to Lapland.'

'I know I do. That's what I said. But how?'

'Fundraising in the garden centre?'

'Keith would never let me. Unless I tell him what I've done, and then he'll sack me.'

'Oh, angel I wish I was there to give you a big hug right now. We'll make a plan when I'm back.'

Juan is due back from Spain in a couple of days...he has been at home to spend time with his parents before Christmas.

'It'll be too late by then,' I say. 'I need a plan now.'

'OK, well - you could write to local companies asking them to donate, write to any rich individuals locally, go door-to-door collecting money. I don't know.'

'Yes. Yes. I'll have to try things like that. Oh, you've cheered me up. I feel better now...I'm going to write to all the big companies in town, and I'll work out where the richest people live and put notes through their doors. You've made me feel a bit better. Thank you.'

'Shall I tell you a joke to really make you feel better,' he says.

'Oh yes - go on.'

'OK. Are you sitting comfortably?'

I walk over to Santa's grotto, situated next to my Christmas area, and settle myself into the main man's big throne-like chair.

'Yes,' I say, as Juan begins to talk.

'Well, there were two men sitting, drinking at a bar at the

top of the Empire State Building. One man, dressed in a Christmas jumper turned to the other man - we'll call him Bob, and said: 'You know, last week I discovered that if you jump from the top of this building, the winds around the building are so intense that by the time you fall to the 10th floor, they will carry you around the building and back into a window'. The bartender shook his head in disapproval and continued to wipe the bar.

'What, are you nuts?' said Bob. 'There's no way that could happen,'

'It's true,' said Christmas jumper man. 'Let me prove it to you,' and he got up from the bar, jumped over the balcony, and plummeted toward the street below. As he neared the 10th floor, the high winds whipped him around the building and back into the 10th floor window and he took the elevator back up to the bar.

Bob was open-mouthed. 'That must have been a onetime fluke. There's no way that could happen again.'

'OK, then I'll prove it again.'

So, the Christmas jumper man leapt out of the window again. Just as he went hurtling toward the street, the 10th floor wind gently carried him around the building and into the window. Once upstairs he urged his fellow drinker to try it.

'Well, why not,' said Bob. 'It clearly works. I'll try it.'

Bob jumped over the balcony and plunged down, passed the 11th, 10th, 9th, 8th floors...and hit the pavement with a loud bang.

Back upstairs, the bartender turned to Christmas jumper man. 'You know, Superman, you're a real jerk when you're drunk.'

'Oh God, that's terrible,' I say. 'But it did distract me for a little while, so thank you.'

'That's OK,' says Juan. 'Just remember - however bad things get, you're better off than poor Bob.'

'I suppose that's one way to look at it.'

'Oh - I've just thought of another joke. Do you want to hear it?'

'Oh yes please,' I say, snuggling down even further into Santa's seat.

'My grandpa has the heart of a lion....and a lifetime ban from the zoo.'

'Na, not as good,' I say.

'OK, I went to a beekeeper to get 12 bees. He counted and gave me 13. 'Sir, you gave me an extra' I told him, but he replied: 'That's a freebie''

'Yeah, I think you might have peaked with the first joke. I'm going to go back to my office now, and have a think about rich people to contact. I'll see you soon. OK?'

Despite what I say to Juan, I don't go straight back to the office. I stay snuggled up in Santa's throne, almost falling asleep in the comfort of the place, as the sound of the Christmas music drifts through. It's only when my phone rings, that I realise I've started to nod off.

I look at my phone. It's an unknown number. I never like to answer unknown numbers in case it's someone very boring, asking me something very boring. Or in case it's the bank. No one wants to risk answering a call from their bank, do they?

But then I realise it will be Juan ringing back. Presumably with another terrible joke.

'Hello my beautiful gay friend, what very unfunny joke are you going to tell me now?' I say, chancing my arm that it's him and not the guy in charge of my bank account, calling to find out why I spend so much money on take-aways.

There's a silence on the end of the phone.

'Come on then, you loser - let's have it.'

Nothing.

'Juan?'

'No, it's David, actually. David Beckham.'

'Holy mother of God. I thought you were someone different.'

Don't worry,' he says in that incredibly familiar tone. I can hear the laugh in the back of his voice.

'I'm just calling because it's Harper's Christmas party tomorrow and we wondered whether you were free to come and decorate her tree again. She loved it so much when you did it last year.'

'Of course,' I say.

'It's late notice because the party is at 3pm tomorrow, so we'll need you here by 10am if possible.'

'Sure, perfect. Of course. I'll be there,' I say.

'Oh great,' he says. 'Victoria thought you'd be busy with all your other clients at this time of year, but if you can fit us in, that would be awesome.'

'Yes, a slot has just become available tomorrow. I can fit you in,' I say. I never said that I was a professional tree dresser, but that's obviously the impression he has.

I look over at the wonder Christmas trees, here at the garden centre, with their Rick Ashley bells hanging on them, and think that - yes - one can imagine how he might confused me with a professional decorator.

David and I say our goodbyes and I let out a large squeal before I run as fast as my chunky legs will carry me, past the nativity scene and towards Keith's office. Mike from bathrooms sees me fly past him at lightning speed and shouts: 'Oy Mary. All the kids are asking why there's an elephant in the manger.'

And you know, his question doesn't even bother me.

'That's what one of the three wise men travelled on,' I pant back, as I tear through the centre like Mo Farrah.

'The three wise men did not travel on elephants - that's complete fantasy,' says Tony the Taps.

'Fantasy? Or perhaps it's elephantasy,' I shout back, laughing very loudly at my own joke. Indeed, so preoccupied am I with my own joke that I go tearing straight into Keith who is emerging from his office with a clipboard and two pot plants. The clipboard drops to the ground, the greenery goes one way and Keith goes the other way.

'What in the name of the lord is all the rush for?' he asks, as I apologise and help him to his feet, patting him down to get rid of the dirt until he rudely pushes my hand away.

'Why were you rushing?'

'Because David Beckham just called. He wants me to come over and decorate a Christmas tree for Harper tomorrow.'

'Holy cow,' says Keith. 'My office. Now.'

Later that evening, Ted and I are sitting on the sofa together. He's watching Curb Your Enthusiasm and laughing a lot. The other thing he's doing a lot is telling me that Larry David is exactly like me. 'Honestly, Mary - look at the chaos he causes. He's so like you.'

'I don't always cause chaos,' I say, but even as I say it, I realise that I'm wrong. I do cause chaos. Like this bloody trip to Lapland. I've written letters to 20 companies and six rich people locally but I haven't posted them because I got worried. What if Oliver's dad doesn't want me to tout his son around to raise money? What if he's a proud man who would find that embarrassing? It's one thing to drop a note into a Christmas Wishes box, quite another thing to hawk your son around to the highest bidder.

'Are you looking forward to going to the Beckhams? You and David are like old friends,' says Ted.

'Yes, we're almost family,' I say. 'Honestly, I sometimes wish David would stop ringing all the time. He's becoming a bit of a nuisance.'

Then I pause for a moment.

'In all honesty, Ted, I'm much more worried about getting this little kid to Lapland than I am about going to the Beckhams. It's really upsetting me that he's having such a difficult time. I think I'm going to pay myself, out of my money. I've got money in my savings account.'

Ted smiles at me. 'You are such an incredible, kind and sweet person. I don't think you have any idea how much I love you, but you really can't pay yourself. You can't, Mary. It wouldn't be right.'

'I don't know,' I say. 'I think it might be the simplest way to get him there.'

CHAPTER 8

18TH DECEMBER

I wake up at 5am and the realisation hits me like a steam train...I'm going to David Beckham's house today. Beckham - you know the guy with the tattoos, plays football, married to a Spice Girl and is the very embodiment of manly beauty? Well - that's where I'm going. Today. Right now.

I went last year and it ended up being an absolute triumph... in the end! But at the beginning - my Gos it was awful. I was terrified. There were all these arty-farty interior designers who were very cross that I had been put in charge of decorating the tree. I shrugged them off and began to embellish the tree in my usual sophisticated manner...you know - flying pink pigs and brightly coloured squeaky animals. Then the designers came and saw what I had done, and had a fit. They ran off to get Victoria, almost apoplectic with rage. My day was saved by the fact that Harper, her daughter, came along and loved the decorations. Posh Spice was delighted that her daughter was happy and all ended well.

Now they have invited me back to do the tree again.

I don't feel as nervous this year because the tree is for Harper's party, and I feel that I know what she likes. I know what sort of 'look' she'll be expecting. I realise that she's a year older, and children change a lot in a year, but I think I've got the measure of her. So this time, instead of fear, it is excitement that is rushing through me.

I get my things ready to go, and slip the letter from Oliver's dad into my bag, along with my savings account details. I'm definitely going to pay for the trip to Lapland myself, and give the little boy the trip of his life. I'll go to the bank after we've done Beckham's tree and sort the whole thing out.

My driver for the day is big Derek who is working with the centre on a three-week contract to help shift Christmas trees around, and to say that he is excited about the prospect of meeting David Beckham would be to completely understate the way he's feeling. I jump up into the cab next to him and he looks at me in amazement. 'Please tell me the truth, the absolute truth. Are we going to David Beckham's house today? Tell me really... Or is this just a wind up. If it's a wind up tell me now before I get any more excited.'

'No, it's not a wind up,' I tell him. 'This is all perfectly above board. I went there last year to do the tree and he's invited me back.'

'I'm his biggest fan,' says Derek, in a voice which is slightly scary.

'David himself might not be there,' I say, eager to dampen the excitement so the poor guy doesn't wet himself or anything.

'But we'll be in his house? Where he lives? I mean... That's amazing.'

'Yes, we will be in his house, and I think Victoria Beckham

will be there to meet us, and Harper – her daughter – should be there, but I'm not sure about David.'

'Do you think they'd mind if I did videos in the house?'

'Yes, I think they would really mind. You can't do anything like that, Derek. You just have to bring the tree in, bring all my stuff in, and help me when I ask you to. You can't be taking pictures or going up and stealing David Beckham's pyjamas, or sniffing his sheets or anything.'

'Okay then,' he says, pulling the van over to the side of the road.

'Why have you stopped?'

'I better take it off Twitter.'

'Take what off Twitter?'

'I put a post up saying that I would be putting up videos giving people guided tours of David Beckham's house. I'll just take him down if you don't think I can do that.'

'Shit, yes – take it down. Why would you think you could do guided tours around Beckham's house?'

'For a laugh,' he says, as he fiddles with his phone, and hopefully removes the various posts he's put up. We seem to be sitting there quite a long time.

'Have you not done it yet?'

'There are about 50 posts on Twitter, Facebook and Instagram,' he says. 'I'm just making sure that I remove them all.'

'Oh dear God, Derek, why would you think that was appropriate?'

He shrugs as he continues to play on his phone, and eventually declares that all the posts are removed.

'Okay, keep going straight down this road then at the roundabout turn left and there is a string of shops along there that sell fabulous Christmas decorations. That's where I'm going.'

'Is that where David Beckham lives?'

'No, Derek, David Beckham doesn't live at the back of a Christmas decoration shop on a scruffy old street in south London. We'll get to Beckham's house, we just need to go and buy the decorations I need first.'

We arrive at the shop and I clamber out of the van and towards the door. I remember so vividly coming here last year, and going over the road to the rather posh Christmas decoration shop, in which the decorations were all laid out like beautiful, expensive jewellery. Or I should say – beautiful, expensive and dull. I'd just about given up last year, and decided that I couldn't find the right ornaments in that shop, when I glanced at the one over the road and realised that was the one for me.

It's a sort of pick-a-mix of decorations, each one costing no more than a pound. For the really cheap and cheerful ones you can get three for £1, but because this is the Beckham's house, we're going for broke and spending a full pound on each glossy little decoration.

This is for Harper's party, so it needs to reflect what she loves in life, and I've been through her Instagram account and found that animals and bracelets feature more than anything else. That might sound like an odd combination, and I don't expect it fully encompasses all her likes and dislikes in the world, but it's certainly what she seems to show most of on Instagram. There are also loads of pictures of her with her dad, hugging him and being carried by him, and generally being a real daddy's girl, so I bear that in mind as I scan the aisles for appropriate decorations.

I go first of all to the bright pink cats with hellishly long whiskers like false eyelashes. Could anything be more perfect? I throw 10 into the baskets, before spotting teddy bears to hang in the tree, they're a mixture of brown and black ones. Black doesn't seem very Christmassy, so 12 brown bears tumble one by one into the basket to nestle down next to the girlish cats. I'll pick up tinsel of course, in a mixture of pink, lilac and white. I'm a bit torn on the white, I think pink and lilac are great, but I throw some white in just in case she's feeling a little more modest this Christmas than last. Then I see some beautiful bracelets in an array of colours. The lovely thing about them is that you hang them in the tree and then friends can come and help themselves to a bracelet that they can wear to go home. I definitely want some of these. They've got 40 in the shop so I throw all of them into my basket, before reaching for candy canes and some sizeable Father Christmases that you hang on the tree and squeeze to hear them say 'Ho Ho Ho.'

Honestly, I'm having an absolute field day. There are huge pink teddy bears. I take one to sit on top of the tree like the star of Bethlehem. Then realise that that might be too unreligious, so I take a star as well, and figure that if the bear is holding the star and then wedged onto the top of the tree with a branch up his bottom, that will look altogether more religious.

I think I've got enough, but I'm never one to under-do things, I'd rather take too much than get there and wish I'd bought more, so I grab handfuls of singing sheep, dancing cows that jiggle and shake when you make a noise, and these crabs that crawl around sideways underneath the tree going round and round with flashy lights. I've never seen anything so ridiculous in my life, so I buy 10 of those. Armed with two carrier bags full of £200 worth of tat, I retreat to the van, and tell Derek we are ready to go. He's been sitting in the cab of the van while I've been choosing ornaments, and has obviously taken the opportunity to spruce himself up a bit. He stinks of something musky and old-fashioned, and his hair has been gelled back, David Beckham style. It's a style that looks perfectly lovely on the former England footballer, but on big Derek who is pushing 60, it looks less alluring.

We drive through the countryside out to the Beckhams' beautiful country retreat, then through the gates and up to the house. Derek is hyperventilating. It's not ideal.

We're greeted at the door by a collection of staff who lead us through and show us where the tree should go. Derek brings it in and I start work.

'Can you pass me the lights I brought from work? The ones called 'pulsating disco stars,' I say.

Derek rummages through the box and hands them to me. I explain how I want them to run through the tree, one on every branch.

'I brought five boxes with us so there should be plenty,' I add.

Derek gets his ladder from the van and begins doing as I've asked. It's quite a big job, and I feel much happier now he's fully occupied, whistling as he carefully attaches the lights as I've asked him to. As long as he's within sight, and working hard, everything should be OK. Can you imagine if he'd gone round the house, videoing the place? We'd have been bloody arrested.

I finish all the decorating in around two hours which everyone seems surprised about. I wonder how long there were expecting it to take? Perhaps it would have looked more impressive if I'd worked really slowly, and made a real meal out of it. I ask whether Harper is available to come and look at the tree so I can talk her through it, and make sure she's happy. The assistants look at me as if I've just asked to meet the queen, but they shuffle off and emerge 20 minutes later to say Harper will be down shortly. It's only a few minutes later that I see Harper, accompanied by David.

There's an embarrassing gasp from Derek, like a teenage girl at a *Take That* concert.

'Stay calm,' I mutter, as he reaches out for the wall to steady himself.

I step forward and introduce myself to David and to Harper, and I tell her all about the tree...I explain that the flashing loops are bagels that she can take off and keep, or invite her friends to help themselves to...I show her the mad creatures running around underneath the tree and lights woven through it.

'It's brilliant,' she says to David. 'I can't wait for my friends to see it.'

David smiles.

'Cup of tea?' he offers.

'I'd love one please,' I say.

David turns to look at Derek. 'Would you like one?' he asks, but Derek has lost the power of speech, and he just stands there, limply leaning against the wall and staring ahead like he's on some psychotic drugs.

'No?' says David. 'OK, well, we'll be through here, in the kitchen, if you change your mind.'

I follow David into the kitchen, as Harper takes my hand. It's the most wonderful feeling in the world, as he skips and smiles and continues to tell me how wonderful the tree is.

'Do you have children?' asks David.

'No, not yet. I'd love to one day,' I say. 'I love kids.' And then, for some reason, I think of Oliver, the little boy with one leg, and I wonder how he got on in hospital and whether he's OK.

And then that reminds me of the trip to Lapland that I have t
sort out...'

'Are you OK?' asks David, and I regret to say, dear readers, I
burst into tears.

'Oh no, have I put my foot in it?' he asks.

'No, not at all, I'm sorry,' I say, and I tell him the whole sad
tale.

He listens, quietly, as I talk, and I tell him that I've decided
to pay for the trip myself.

'Don't do anything for the next hour,' he says. 'Let me make
a couple of calls and I'll come back to you.'

'Really?'

'Yes, I'll try and help you.'

Before we leave, I get pictures of David, Harper and me in
front of the tree, and various shots of the different decorations.
I know I'll need pictures for when I put together the press
releases this afternoon.

Then I lift Derek off the wall and lead him to the van.

Before we head off, I do a quick interview with a local news
reporter, at the end of the road leading to the Beckham's house.
Then, it's time to leave.

'Come on, let's go back to Fosters,' I say, as he starts up the
engine and we hit the road. We're about five minutes into the
journey when one of the guys from work rings him.

'Oh it was brilliant,' I listen to him saying, 'I was chatting
away to David, we got on really well. Poor Mary was a bit over-
awed, but I was totally cool. I think David and I will stay in
touch for a very long time.'

'Really?' I say. 'Am I going to have to listen to you telling
everyone how you and David got on like a house on fire?'

But before he can answer, my phone rings.

'Mary, it's David,' says a familiar voice. 'I just wanted to tell you that I've sorted out that trip for you...for the little boy without a leg. A man called Michael Foley will call you this afternoon.'

'What?'

'You told me about the little boy who wanted to go to Lapland? Well, my manager has contacted a company that will give you a free trip - for the kid and his parents and for you and a guest. For a few days before Christmas. And I'll come to the airport to meet him when you return. But don't tell him that bit, then it'll be a nice surprise for him.'

'Oh God, I love you,' I shout. 'You have no idea what this means. If you ever leave Victoria, please will you marry me?'

'Well, um, I. I'm not really planning to leave Victoria.'

'I know but it was worth a shot.'

'So, you'll tell the little boy's mum and dad?'

'Yes, I will,' I reply. He doesn't have a mum, but I'll tell the dad. 'Thank you so much. Honestly, this is just wonderful. I think I'm going to cry.'

I put the phone down and smile to myself. I'll go back to the office now and sort everything out - the date on Saturday, a press release about today, and the amazing Lapland trip for the beginning of next week. Bloody hell, Christmas is starting to come together.

CHAPTER 9

19TH DECEMBER

It's 6 am on a freezing cold morning, and I am at Heathrow Airport to pick up Juan. My gorgeous little friend has been in Spain to visit his relatives for a few days but now he's coming back where he belongs.

Ted is outside waiting in the car while I scan the airport. As usual, I don't need to look too closely amongst all the grey suits and blue coats for Juan, as he strides into view in a gorgeous bright pink silky looking jacket and zebra print trousers. He struts when he walks, treating every piece of pavement like a catwalk. He is such a magnificent creature. I wish I had an ounce of his style and confidence.

'I'm here!' I shout, prompting him to swing round and give me the biggest smile as he runs towards me and hugs me tightly. He doesn't do that thing that they do in the movies where he picks me up into the air and spins me round. He tried to do that once and almost broke his back, so we just stick to hugging these days.

'You look gorgeous, darling,' I say, stroking the jacket which does feel exactly like silk.

'It was a Christmas present from my sister, isn't it fabulous?' he says. 'She said she might come over and visit in the New Year. Would that be okay?'

'Oh my God, of course. It would be absolutely lovely to meet her.'

This isn't entirely true. It wouldn't be at all lovely to meet her because I've seen photographs of her and she's absolutely bloody gorgeous. I could do without her swishy dark ponytail and long, tanned limbs striding around my flat first thing in the morning.

We get out of the car when we reach mine, and Ted zooms off straight away, like he's just done some sort of drug deal. 'I've got a meeting first thing, sorry - I have to fly,' he says, before Lewis Hamiltoning it down the road.

I put my bag on the sofa and go into the kitchen to make coffee. All the while, my phone is beeping and vibrating non-stop. I know what it is, it's all the tweets and Facebook messages after the Beckham tree thing yesterday. We put together a press release yesterday afternoon and attached the picture that I took, and it was on most of the newspaper websites last night.

'Why is your phone ringing so much?' he asks. 'Do you want me to answer it?'

'No, don't worry. It's just because I went to decorate David Beckham's Christmas tree and all the papers ran stories about it this morning.'

'David Beckham? What? 'You decorated David Beckham's tree? Oh my God. Oh my God. Is he gorgeous? Is he absolutely bloody gorgeous?'

'Yes, yes and yes. And you haven't heard the best bit - I was going to tell you when we go out for a drink later, but I can't wait any longer.'

'What?'

'He's sorted out the trip to Lapland. He's found someone to sponsor it so that Oliver and his dad can go.'

'No way. We need to go somewhere really swanky for breakfast to celebrate,' says Juan. 'That's amazing.'

'I can't do breakfast. I'm working this morning, but why don't you come to the store for 3pm when I finish, and we can go out then, have a few drinks, and catch up properly.'

'OK,' he says, 'But I want all the details then, every one of them...'

'You will have them, my love, I promise you.'

It's 7.30 before I get to work, despite my official start time being 7am today. Luckily Keith always works nine till six, so doesn't have a clue what time I get to the office. I go in, switch on my computer, and check the newspapers online to see what they've said about the Christmas tree.

Wow. The picture is everywhere. Every site I can think of is running the picture of beautiful David with his pretty grin, standing next to my tree. The only horror is how big I look. I know I should just be glad of all I've achieved, and revel in the moment of glory but I am literally twice as wide as David Beckham. And he's a big bloke. I'm also half his height. I really wish I hadn't stood next to him for the photo now.

I've got to lose weight. Somehow. I know this is the wrong time of year for worrying about that, but as I look at myself in the picture, I feel a tear creep into the back of my eye. The only thing that distracts me, and stops me staring at the hideous picture of myself is a loud banging on the office window.

I look up to see around a dozen people staring into the office. They cheer when I look up. 'It's Mary Christmas,' shouts one, which makes me laugh.

'How was David Beckham?' shouts another.

'Wonderful,' I say.

Blimey, it's only 8am, the doors have only just opened and a fan club has formed. I look back at the pictures and think - yeah, I need to lose weight, and - yeah - I do look big in those, but for heaven's sake, I'm getting some things right. I wave at them which elicits another big cheer and a spontaneous round of applause.

I thank them, and I turn back to my computer but can sense that they are all still out there, so I decide to head into the staff cafeteria to study the coverage on my phone. There's a ripple of applause as I walk in, and they present me with a free caramel latte and a chocolate donut.

Christ. Now I'm going to be three times the size of David Beckham.

I click onto Twitter to find it aglow with discussion about my tree. There are a few unkind comments, and a few references to my weight of course.

I'm surprised there were any candy canes left says Gal3345 from Leeds.

Wow! Have you seen the size of the woman who decorated it? says Peter from Barnsley.

Good grief, she's never turned down a pudding, has she? says Mandy from Bath.

It's hard to read things like that about yourself, but - all in all - it's criticism I can handle because what these unkind commentators don't realise I say far worse things to myself about my weight than they ever could.

The positive PR for the store is great, with lots of mentions of the various departments and how we've been reaching out to the community through our *Christmas Post-box of Wishes and Dreams*. Yes! I knew it was worth sending out press releases. Keith may have mocked the idea that global media would cover us but - look at this - they have. They even have the good grace not to mock the inclusion of an elephant in the manger.

It's around 20 minutes before Keith bursts in and shouts 'You Beauuuuty!' like he's cheering a goal scorer at a football match. 'The place is packed. It's bloody packed.'

'I have more good news. David Beckham helped find someone to sponsor Oliver's trip to Lapland.'

'The kid with one leg?'

'Yes. I'm going too. I hope that's OK. Just for a couple of days to make sure it all goes smoothly.'

'Of course that's OK. Of course. Anything. Anything at all... more donuts?'

'No, I'm OK for donuts, but it would be great if someone could go out and empty the Post Box of Wishes & Dreams for me. I can't really go outside or I'll get mobbed.'

'Of course, of course,' he says, running straight outside to do my bidding. I love how he didn't even react to my description of it as the *Post Box of Wishes & Dreams*.

Keith rushes in with the notes he's found. There a few notes requesting different tin sizes in the paint and suggesting that we do wider planks of wood, then there are ones from kindly people wishing us all a Merry Christmas, wishing for world peace, and generally saying nice things about the world. At the bottom there is a letter, clearly written by a child.

. . .

Dear Christmas Elf,

For Christmas I would like:
   One. Sticks
   Two. More sticks
   Three. Even more sticks.

PS I really like sticks

From,
   Jamie Mason, aged five.

I'm overcome with joy that there is a task here that I could actually fulfil. It would be no effort at all for me to go along tonight with piles of sticks for this young kid. And I know exactly the man to come and do it with me.

'You want me to what?' says Juan. 'I thought we were going to have a few beers and talk about David Beckham.'

'Yes, we will go to the pub, have a few beers and a bite to eat, then around 6 o'clock we will go to the house and leave loads of sticks outside with a note saying they're from the gardening centre for Jamie and we hope the whole family has a very lovely Christmas.

'Don't you think that will be a nice thing to do? Go and get him loads of sticks?'

'Go on then, I'm in,' says Juan, wearily. 'Shall I come to the garden centre for 3 o'clock as we planned?'

'I'll see you then,' I say, as I put the phone down and scan through the messages that have been left on my phone.

There's a message from the Lebanese takeaway, confirming the delivery of lunch for the grand date, then about 20 requests for newspaper interviews from all over the world. Then there is one from Michael Foley, David Beckham's assistant. He tells me the trip has been organised and we will be leaving on 22nd, coming back on 24th. 'See your emails,' he writes. 'All the details and tickets are in there.'

Oh brilliant! I forget about the interview requests from papers in China, Outer Mongolia and Luxemburg, and rush to my emails. There it all is. There are all details of the cab that will pick us up and take us to the airport, the hotel details and photos of Santa galore. There's a separate email for me to forward to Oliver's dad, Brian, so I do that, and go back to the email for me: there are pictures of reindeer on snowy plains, huskies, gorgeous food and pretty people in bobble hats. I need a bobble hat. Where can I get a bobble hat?

CHAPTER 10

STILL 19TH DECEMBER

*J*uan and I cling onto one another as we stagger towards the small cottage, nestled in a quiet cul de sac off Cobham High Street. Oh dear. I can't walk very straight, and everything's just a little bit blurry. We drank way more than we'd meant to in the pub, I'll be honest with you. We were only going for a couple, but there was such a lot of catching up to do, and then we were celebrating the whole Beckham thing and the trip to Lapland, so a couple of drinks turned into five or six and by the end of it all, well - not to put too fine a point on it - I feel very drunk.

I guess we should have just staggered off home to sleep it all off, but instead we've staggered our way to this pretty cottage in which the boy who wants sticks lives.

The two of us now stand in front of the beautifully decorated house, with the lovely big wreath on the door, and sparkly lights around the window frames. You can see the orange glow behind the heavy curtains, indicating that the lights are on inside. They're in. Now we need to provide them with sticks.

I notice that Juan is swaying a little. Or perhaps I'm swaying: it's hard to know. There is certainly a lot of swaying going on.

'OK, come on then,' I say to Juan. I can hear myself slur and I notice how glassy his eyes look...you know that look people have when they've drunk too much? Well, he has it. Big time.

'Sshhhh...' he says, waving his finger in front of his face. 'We have to be quiet now.'

'Yes,' I whisper so quietly that he can barely hear me. 'Now we know where the house is, let's go into the park over there and collect the sticks which we can leave on the doorstep. Yeah?'

Juan just nods. I'm not sure he knows what I'm saying. He staggers along behind me as we try to walk towards the park. 'Have you got the letter with you - the letter for the little boy?'

'Of course,' I say, pulling the letter out of my pocket.

Dear Jamie,

Here are some sticks from Foster's gardening centre. I really hope you enjoy playing with them.

I know you love sticks, so hopefully these will be a Christmas treat. I hope you and your family have a lovely time over Christmas.

Lots of love.

From,

Mary Brown and everyone working at Foster's DIY & gardening centre.

. . .

We start gathering as many sticks as we can carry, bundling them into black bags and tipping them onto the doorstep.

I'll be honest, it looks like we've just tipped out a whole heap of rubbish on their doorstep, but once they read the letter, and remember the note that their son wrote, they'll be pleased that we took the time to do this.

I smile at Juan. What five-year-old wouldn't be delighted to come out of his house and see all this?' I say. 'I think we've made a kid very happy.'

'And you could make a 35-year-old very happy if you would accompany him back to Cobham High Street for another cheeky pint before we head home.

'Good thinking,' I say, as I see the curtain move slightly in the house, as if someone is aware of our presence. 'Let's get out of here.'

The two of us power-walk (power stagger might be more accurate) away from the house, eventually, breaking into a mild jog, as we hear a sound behind us, then we go racing down the little country lane, which leads back to the centre of Cobham, laughing hysterically as we go. We emerge onto the High Street and give each other a high five, before pausing to catch our breath.

'I think that was a really cool thing to do.'

'It was. That kid is not going to believe it when his mum and dad show him all the sticks.'

'I know. It would be great to be there to see his face when he realises they are all for him.'

'You know you are covered in leaves and bits of broken branches, don't you? All over your jumper. Look at you...you're filthy' As Juan says this, he looks down and sees that his own jumper is covered in bits.

'Oh Christ, I look like a vagrant,' he says, frantically brushing himself down, before picking off the remaining bits of debris, and starting to help me.

'How have you got so much more than me on you?' he asks.

'There's a bigger expanse of jumper to attract leaves,' I reply, as he plucks bits off me like a cat grooming its kittens.

'Done,' he says, rubbing his hands together to remove the last vestiges of the rubble from his fingers.

'Come on then,' I say. 'It'll be last orders soon.' We start to move towards the pub door when a police car comes zooming towards us at top speed with its lights going and it's nee naw nee naw nee naw blaring out.

'Someone's in trouble,' I say to Juan, as it screeches to a stop next to us. 'Those boys don't look like they're messing around.'

We stand and watch for a minute as an officer jumps out of the car and runs towards us. I step aside to let them enter the pub, but the officer stops in front of me.

'Don't go in there,' he says.

'I'm not. I was opening it for you.'

'Come over to the police car,' says the officer. Juan lingers by the pub door. 'You too, sir.'

Another officer steps out of the car as we approach it, and the two of them stand in front of us., looking at us as if we're hardened criminals.

'We've had reports of two individuals hanging around in front of a house in Rose Avenue, before dumping a load of gardening rubbish. The people described to us look very much like you.'

'Yes, it was us,' I say. 'Not loitering or anything. We weren't causing any trouble. We just dropped off a load of sticks.'

'You dumped a load of branches and mud on the doorstep.'

'Yes. Not mud - not really - we were mainly trying to put sticks there.'

'You dumped your gardening waste on their doorstep instead of taking it to a dump or disposing of it in the proper manner. That's fly tipping. You also frightened the lady of the house by loitering outside in what she describes as 'a loud, drunken manner.'

'No, we didn't. No, you've got it all wrong,' I try. 'That's not what happened at all.'

'So, you didn't dump leaves, sticks and branches outside Mandarin Cottage on Rose Avenue around 20 minutes ago? Because I have descriptions here which match you...a fat, unkempt woman with messy hair and an effeminate looking man who was jigging around constantly like he needed the toilet. Would you say that was an accurate description?'

'It's a bit harsh,' I said. 'My hair's OK, isn't it?'

'Did you or didn't you dump rubbish outside their house?'

'Yes we did, but as a gift.'

'A gift.'

'They were sticks for Jamie, the little boy who lives there. Jamie wrote to me and asked me whether he could have loads of sticks for Christmas, so we put them there as a present. We left a note with them.

As I mention the note, it occurs to me that I don't recall leaving the note. I push my hand into my pockets and feel it in there, I pull it out and open it.

'Didn't you leave it with the sticks?' says Juan. It's the first time he's spoken since the police arrived. 'And - by the way - I wasn't jigging around like I needed the loo, I was just cold, that's all.'

I look up at the officer, and show him my note. He begins

reading it while I delve into my handbag, and pull out the note that the kid sent to us in the *Christmas Post Box of Wishes and Dreams*. I hand that over as well.

'The family didn't know why you'd dumped a load of sticks outside the property,' he says. 'It was an unwise thing to do even with the note. Could you not have spoken to the lady first?'

'Sorry,' I say, looking down at the floor as he speaks.

'Come with us,' he says. 'We'll go back to the cottage and you can explain.'

Juan and I get into the police car, glancing at one another nervously.

'Are we going to have to put all those bloody sticks back?' Juan whispers. I just shrug. I didn't know, but it seems likely.

We pull up outside the house and the officer knocks on the cottage door. A miserable woman with short, badly dyed hair answers.

'That's them,' she shouts, pointing aggressively in my direction. 'They're the ones...'

The police officer steps forward and explains the misunderstanding. I stand there fiddling with my hair. Why did she describe it as messy? I don't have messy hair. Her hair is horrible. How dare she.

The lady looks at the letters and at a little boy, sitting on the sofa.

'Jamie, come here and see what these people have brought for you,' she says, bending over to gather a handful of the sticks.'

Jamie takes one look and lets out an almighty shriek: 'Sticks!' He gathers them into his arms, smiles at Juan and me and settles down to arrange them in what seems like order of size.

'I'm sorry that we panicked,' says the lady. 'But I saw you

hanging around outside and when I came out and saw all the mess, I was shocked. A police car was driving down the road so I flagged the officers down.'

'It's OK, we were just trying to be Christmassy,' I say. 'I'm in charge of Christmas at the store. I decorated David Beckham's tree yesterday.'

Oh God. The lady looks from me to the officers, while her husband, sitting quietly on their brown sofa for the duration of the chat, just coughs gently to himself, as if passing a warning to her that I am clearly nuts.

'Why don't you stay for a drink,' says the woman.

'Sure,' I say. 'That's really nice of you.'

'I was talking to the officers, actually, but you're welcome to stay too.'

Her husband coughs again, as if to warn her about the dangers of allowing two raving nutters into the house.

But the lady is not perturbed. She leaves the room and her husband flicks on the television so he doesn't have to converse with us. Then she returns with a tray full of glasses. 'It's a little drop of brandy,' she says, handing out the glasses.

'Good heavens!' shouts her husband, forcing his poor wife to jump.

'What's the matter? It's only the cheap brandy, not the expensive stuff.'

'No, I mean - look - on the television.'

We all look passed Julie and her tray of drinks to the television behind her where I stand, in all my festive glory, outside the Beckhams' house. He turns the volume up and they listened as I speak about how - for the second year running - I have decorated the Beckhams' Christmas tree.

They all look at me, awe-struck.

'I told you before that I decorated his tree.'

'What's her house like?' asks the lady, while Jamie hugs his sticks, and her husband stares open-mouthed at the screen.

'Nice,' I say. 'A really nice house.'

CHAPTER 11

20TH DECEMBER

I look out of the window to see a perfect winter's morning: crisp, fresh and lovely: an ideal day on which to meet the man of your dreams.

'Surprise, surprise,' I sing out in the semi darkness as Ted stirs beside me.

'I'm Cilla Black,' I add, in case he didn't get the Cilla reference from the song.

'Good for you' he says, moving as if he's going to roll over and go back to sleep, but then he sits up and stares at me through sleepy eyes. His face is stubbly, his hair is all standing on end and he scratches his chest hair like a baboon.

'Why are you Cilla? Are you about to do something ridiculous, like take to the stage at the Royal Variety Performance, or develop a Liverpudlian accent?'

'No. I'm organising the blind date today... Like Cilla Black did. You remember her program 'Blind Date'?'

'Oh, I'd forgotten all about that. You've worked five days this week, do you have to work Saturday as well? Can they not just get on with the date without you? Do you have to be there?'

'I always have to be there when Christmas calls,' I say, standing on the bed as if preparing to give a Martin Luther King type speech. 'Christmas doesn't confine itself to the days in the week, Christmas is everywhere Christmas is all of us. When I am wanted for Christmas-related activities, I must go. I'm a bit like Father Christmas in that respect. And now I must leave...'

'Good God,' says Ted, pulling the duvet over his head and snuggling back down into it while I dance into the bathroom to prepare myself for the exciting day ahead.

As I sit on the bus into work, I think through everything I need to get done before this wonderful Christmas date. I've asked the guys from the warehouse to move the pagoda into the main area by the Christmas nativity scene and to have the beautiful Christmas trees, now decked out in the same decorations as the Beckham tree, lined up to create an alleyway of Christmas trees leading up to their lunch table.

Then Mandy will run flowers, both real and artificial, through the pagoda (without making it look too much like a wedding scene), and in the middle of it all will be a table and chairs beautifully laid out with linen, crockery, and cutlery that we sell in the store. Keith is very worried about us damaging the things we use, but I've tried to tell him that if we don't use things from the store, a valuable PR opportunity will be lost. I can't lay the table with crockery from Marks and Spencer, can I?

There should be a lot of press interest, certainly a lot of newspapers have been ringing the store to check the timings today. It's a good Christmassy story and it's a bit of fun. It's hard to see what could go wrong really. If Belinda isn't interested in him, or if he isn't interested in Belinda, then they just don't contact one another again and they have had a free meal. Everyone's a winner.

By 12.30pm everything is ready in advance of our 1pm sit down. I never expected it to look quite so fantastic. Ted, and Juan have even come down to support me, and I've managed to persuade Juan to act as waiter for the day.

At five to one, a rather handsome man approaches me. He must be late 30s, I guess, and has a lovely rugged look giving him a film star quality.

'Can I talk to someone about this date today?' he says, and I feel as if all my wishes have come true. Here is Daniel and he's bloody lovely. I smile over at Belinda and see her go a deep shade of tomato.

This man is seriously yummy. She must be delighted.

'Of course,' I say to the man and I hear Belinda giggling in the background. The familiar sound of Juan's voice saying, 'I would', makes me smile. It's all going to be OK. The thing I was most worried about was what Daniel would be like. Now here he is. Ah. All panic over.

'Can you tell me what this date is all about?' he asks. 'I've received information to be here for one o'clock. But I'm a little bit baffled. I'll be honest.'

'Oh my goodness. Come on, Daniel. Please don't worry about a thing,' I say, as I guide him to the table and chairs, laid out so beautifully. 'You are going to have the most wonderful date with a wonderful woman. I signal for Belinda to come over, and she sashays across.

'Let me introduce you to your date for today. This is Belinda,' I say, standing back and opening my arms out to introduce the couple.'

'There's been some terrible mistake.' he says. 'I'm not Daniel. I'm Tom. The date isn't for me. The person who put the note into the box was my son.'

With that, a young boy walks out looking a bit shell-shocked, to be honest. 'How do you mean, your son put the note in the box? I sent emails confirming everything and checking it was all OK,'

'Yes, and you sent them to him, but he's seven, so he doesn't really know what a date is. He's obviously seen it mentioned on some tv programme. I didn't know anything about it until this morning when he asked to be taken to the centre for his date with a lady.'

This is a bloody disaster. I look over at Belinda who is smiling to herself as she waits to join her man at the table. Except her 'man' isn't a man at all, he's a young boy.'

'But I asked his age,' I say.

'No you didn't. He showed me all the emails this morning. You double-checked that he wasn't over 40, and he confirmed that he wasn't.'

Shit.

Daniel has walked over, and is standing next to Belinda who looks confused by the sudden arrival of a young boy. Meanwhile, the photographers start to take pictures.

'Are you single?' I ask Daniel's father.

'No, I am not, I'm married.'

'Are you happily married though?' I try.

'Yes thank-you.'

'You wouldn't fancy a date with a lovely lady?'

'No, I most definitely wouldn't.'

Damn. OK. I need to act.

'Daniel, would you like a free Christmas tree? One just like David Beckham's?' I say to the boy. Daniel nods so I move him away from the date area, signalling for his father to follow us. I lead them over to where the Christmas trees are being sold, and tell the guys there to give him any tree he wants. Then I shake hands with his father, and apologise for the confusion.

Belinda is now looking very worried. Oh God. The poor woman's got enough on her hands with her mum's dodgy boyfriend fancying her, the last thing she needs is to be romantically linked with a seven-year-old and then have it blasted all over the press.

'Are you OK?' asks Ted. 'You look worried.'

'Oh my God, you have to help me. I'm going to ask a massive favour.'

'Sure, go ahead,' he says. 'Ask me anything.'

'Will you please pretend you're the one who's on the date with Belinda and have lunch for the photographers.'

'What?'

'Pretend to be her date. The real date turned out to be a seven-year-old and I don't know what to do.'

'A seven-year-old?' says Belinda, joining the conversation.

'I'm really really sorry,' I say. 'I promise to make it up to you.'

'Come on,' says Ted, grabbing a rose from the pagoda, presenting it to her and walking her towards the table and chairs.

'Sorry for all the confusion, ladies and gentlemen,' I announce, as the two of them take their seats. 'I'd like to introduce you to Ted and Belinda who are going on the Christmas blind date today. They're available for any interviews or questions, then I think we should leave them alone to enjoy their date.'

There are a few questions which Ted battles through before the couple are allowed to sit and enjoy their food, a rather lovely spread from the local restaurant.

Once they are seated and Juan is serving them, I back away from the scene, drop my head into my hands and wonder how I have managed to get this so very bloody wrong. I should have rung the guy and checked him out properly, but all the distractions of Beckham and Lapland...I didn't do the work on this that I should have and I'm really cross with myself. I'm quietly sitting there, while my boyfriend enjoys lunch with another woman when there's a tap on my shoulder.

'Excuse me, do I know you?' asks a slightly familiar looking man.

'I don't think so. Although you do look familiar. I work in the centre here. Perhaps you have seen me here?'

It's bound to be a David Beckham fan wanting to hear more about his idol, but I can't face any of that right now.

'No, I know where I saw you. You're the lady who walked up to our car last week and lay across the bonnet just as I was trying to leave the centre.'

'What?' says Keith. He's confused enough about the sudden change of man on the date, and he doesn't quite understand why there appeared to be a young boy there at one stage. Now this...

'Oh, right. Yes. Ah, I'm glad you brought that up, because that was a complete misunderstanding. I got you mixed up with someone else. Can you believe it? Many apologies.'

'It was strange. You just lay there pouting at me,' said the man, warming to his theme. 'I couldn't work out what was going on. Really - it was the strangest situation, wasn't it, Emma?'

The woman with him nods. 'We thought you were dead at one point because you didn't move at all. Our son, Jacob was really scared.'

'Yes, well - that's terrible. So sorry. Have you got everything you want in the centre today? Can anyone help you with anything?'

'No, we're fine,' says the man, and Keith looks at me quizzically while the two of them walk off.

'I hope you know what you're doing,' he says.

'Yes, of course I do. I thought the date went well. Didn't you?'

'I don't know,' says Keith. 'I don't know at all. That's your boyfriend up there having lunch with her. I really don't know what is happening.'

CHAPTER 12

21ST DECEMBER

'Where are you going now? I thought we might have a lie in this morning before getting ourselves all packed for our trip to Lapland tomorrow,' says Ted.

'I'm just heading into the office to empty the *Post Box of Wishes and Dreams* to see whether there's anything that needs actioning, because I won't be able to do anything for the next few days while we're away, and then by the time we get back from our lovely trip it will be Christmas Eve. If there's something in there that needs dealing with, I should go and deal with it now.'

'OK,' says Ted. 'But everything you seem to 'deal with' from that bloody post box brings trouble. Just be careful, OK? Don't get yourself arrested or beaten up trying to look after people, and particularly don't drag me into any more of your plans.'

'OK, I promise,' I say.

'And don't be long.'

'I'll be as quick as I can. I think Juan's going to come with me and help me move some of the things around because Keith wants the Christmas trees to have a more prominent position in the shop after the Beckham stories.'

'Juan can't move Christmas trees around; he can barely lift up a bunch of flowers. If there's heavy lifting to be done, I'd better come.'

Ted throws the duvet off and scratches his balls. He's a joy in the morning, really, he is.

'There are guys in the shop who can move them. Honestly, there's no need to come unless you really want to.'

I jump in the shower, get myself dressed in casual clothes and wander into the sitting room to see whether Juan is up yet.

He's sitting there on the sofa, painting his toenails a rather horrible shade of green...not a lovely emerald or soft turquoise, but a colour that makes him look like he's got gangrene.

'Why?' I say.

'I thought it would work well and look great with khaki trousers, but now I'm not so sure.'

'No. Not great timing either - we're about to go out.'

Juan insists that it's fine: he'll wear flip flops. It's freezing cold but he doesn't seem put off by the idea of getting frostbite. And, anyway, don't toes that get frostbite go gangrenous? He's short circuited the whole thing by painting them the colour of gangrene in the first place.

'There's no point painting my nails if no one can see them, is there?' he says as he grabs flip-flops, shades and his man bag and sashays towards the door as if he's going to the beach.

We jump onto the bus and head for work. I'm quite nervous about going in today after the fiasco yesterday, but I'm fairly sure that Keith won't be there, and by the time he sits me down and talks to me about it, I'll have been to Lapland and got the best PR possible for the gardening centre so he'll have nothing but praise.

As we walk past Big Terry, who's moving the Christmas trees away from where they were placed yesterday, flanking the romantic meal, to a prominent position in the centre, I'm filled with excitement about everything again. This place does look great.

There's a big sign saying: Want your tree designed like Beckham's? Take a look at this and talk to the staff about how you can copy it at home.

The date may have been far from perfect yesterday but we just about got away with it and I'm sure the photos will look good and highlight the merchandise for sale in the store, and I did manage to decorate Beckham's tree, so it hasn't all been bad. And - of course - I'm taking the lovely Oliver to Lapland tomorrow. It's definitely been a Christmas to remember.

'Juan - do you mind just going over to the post box and taking out the letters in it,' I say, as I help put the decorations back onto the trees, they've moved so clumsily that half of them have tumbled off.

'If there are too many letters to carry, there's a carrier bag in my handbag.'

Juan goes to the post box while I reassemble the decorations.

'One bag enough?' I ask him, as he returns.

'Err...yes,' he says. 'There's only one letter in there.'

'What? I thought there would be loads yesterday after the date. I expected it to be full to bursting.'

'Yeah, perhaps it will be next week?' he suggests.

Juan hands me the solitary letter, from a lady called Agnes who is writing to the good people of Foster's garden centre to thank them for making it so Christmassy and lovely every year. She says that it's a real treat for her to see how full of Christmas spirit the shop is. 'It's been the best place to go at Christmas,' she writes.

Ah, that's lovely. I find myself feeling genuinely pleased that we can bring such joy and happiness into the lives of our customers. I think it's an important thing to do. She goes on to say that she has a present that she would like to give to the person responsible for making the store look so special. And she urges whoever it is to come to the house that evening to receive it.

'Oh God, I'm not going to any more customers' houses,' says Juan. 'Not on your life. Not after stick-gate. That was awful. I think we should keep right away from the homes of the customers.'

'I don't know. I think it might be nice to pop round.'

'Have you forgotten that last time we did that we ended up in the back of a police car? Just write a kind letter back to them thanking them, but telling them we don't accept presents at Christmas.'

'You speak for yourself,' I tell Juan. 'I'm all about receiving presents at Christmas. Isn't that the main point of Christmas? I think we should go there, meet the customer, be nice to her, and graciously accept the present. After all, it's what she wants to do.'

'I guess,' says Juan. 'But you got to be a bit careful about these people. There are some right nutters out there. And I bet among the nuttiest of all are the people who contact the staff of the local gardening centre and invite them around for a 'present'.

'She lives about five minutes from my flat. Why don't we just pop around there later. I'll feel better if we actually respond to as many letter writers as we can.'

'OK, it's your shout. But I'm not coming.'

'What you mean you're not coming? You're my little partner in crime.'

'Yeah, exactly. That's why I'm not coming. See if Ted wants to go.'

'Oh yeah, Ted's really going to want to come and knock on some woman's door.'

'No - this is what I'm saying. He won't want to, and neither do it.'

At 7pm that evening, Juan and I head towards the house belonging to the lady who put the letter into the post-box. He didn't take much convincing, as I knew he wouldn't. I think he secretly likes all the adventures I take him on.

He does make me lead the way, though, so I stride up to the front door and knock gently. It says in the letter that her name is Agnes, but she likes to be called Mrs A.B. Walters. I hate to call people Mr or Mrs. It reminds me too much of school. But I don't want to upset her, so when she opens the door, I am reduced to calling her Mrs Walters, and I explain to her that I am in charge of Christmas at the gardening centre and I just wanted to thank her very much for her note, and how kind I thought it was of her to take the trouble to write in.

'Oh, do come in. I've got some cookies here. Have some cookies.'

'They could be poisoned. This house is weird,' says Juan

who is hiding behind me the whole time. From over my shoulder, I see him scanning the place, like he's my security detail or something. We're invited to sit down and told to eat some cookies. Not offered them, but told to eat them. I nibble nervously on the edge of one while Juan's action man eyes scan the place.

The thing is, the cookies are delicious. They are really lovely. Any latent fears about my safety are swept away by the sweet taste of delicious, crumbly biscuit.

'This is for you,' says Mrs Walters, smiling in quite an odd way. I guess she must be around 60 but could be a lot younger. It's hard to tell. She's wearing an old-fashioned apron and her house looks like it's from the 1960s, mainly brown and with very old-fashioned furniture. Quite awful.

I sit there, wondering what is 'for me' because she hasn't handed me anything. Then she rushes out of the front room and into the kitchen where I hear rustling paper.

Juan and I stare at the big old television while we wait. I notice there are cuckoo clocks everywhere. I mean *everywhere*. How bizarre is that? It's quarter to six and I know we have to get out of the place before 6pm because it'll be mayhem when they all start bursting out of their little wooden houses and cuckooing.

Mrs W is back in the room, and she hands me a parcel wrapped so badly that it looks as if a pet terrier did it. I take it and smile. Just as her husband walks in through the door.

'Oh my my, we have visitors. Who do we have here then?' he asks. 'We weren't expecting visitors. You've given them my favourite biscuits as well.'

'My name is Mary, I work for Foster's gardening centre and your wife sent a kind letter in, thanking us for the way we had decorated the garden centre at Christmas. I just came to wish her a Merry Christmas.'

I look at Mrs Walters, and she's gone scarlet and is mouthing something to me behind her husband's back. When he goes into the porch to hang his raincoat up, she darts over to me and tells me to hide the present. 'Hide the present, quickly. HIDE IT,' she shrieks. 'Don't let him see it.'

I push the present into my handbag. Juan is glaring at me as if to say - *we all knew this would happen. I told you, they're mad.*

When her husband comes back into the room, he looks at us as if he's surprised we're still there.

'Well, we must be off,' I say. 'Merry Christmas to you both.'

'Merry Christmas,' says Mrs M. 'From me and Malcolm.'

We walk outside and she closes the door behind us.

'That was odd. Seriously, there is something wrong there. I don't know what, but something was weird. Do you think she's mental or something?'

'I don't know,' I say. 'She told us to come round but her husband clearly didn't want us there.'

'Perhaps it was a cry for help?' suggests Juan. 'Look at what the present is.'

I pull the bundle of scrunched up paper out of my handbag, and take the wrapping paper off. Inside is some sort of remote control.

'What on earth is that for?'

'I don't know. It doesn't look new. It looks like any normal household remote control,' says Juan, as he leans over and presses a few buttons to see what happens. As he presses, there's a loud shout from Malcolm on the sofa in the sitting room.

'Stop it,' he says.

I press another button and he shouts again.

'It's a remote control to work Malcolm,' says Juan.

Through the window we see Mrs Walters come in from the kitchen.

'Why does this TV keep going on and off?' he says.

'Oh fuck. It's their tv remote control,' says Juan, rather too loudly. Mr Walters looks through the window and spots us both standing there, just as I press the button again and the TV volume raises until it's bellowing out.

'Turn it down,' says Juan, but I can't remember which button I pressed and we're in the semi darkness and I can't see anything.

Malcolm comes out of his house and stands there with arms folded.

'What on earth are you doing?' he shouts, over the sound of people shouting on his television. 'Why are you standing there with our remote control, pressing all the different channels and moving the volume up and down?'

'I don't know,' I say, because I can see his wife in the background and she is shaking her head viciously indicating that she doesn't want us to talk to him at all.

'Is this your idea of fun?' he barks at Juan. 'You: the man with the flip flops and the green toes. Why are your toes green?'

'Oh, I painted them.'

'Did you steal our remote control so you could ruin my evening's television watching?'

'No,' says Juan, giving me a look of pure helplessness.

'Well, what are you doing with it then?'

Agatha is apoplectic now, jumping around behind him, begging us not to reveal that she gave it to us as a Christmas present.

'I don't know what's going on here. I have a good mind to call the police,' he says.

'Oh no. Not the police. Not again,' says Juan, which does nothing to make us look like the innocent party in all this.

'I'm sorry. There's been a misunderstanding. Here's your remote control. I'm very sorry,' I say, handing over the control.

He's just about to bark something back at us when the neighbour pops her head out of her door and shouts over to Malcolm to please turn the television down.

'I'm sorry, Emma,' he says. 'These two nutters from the garden centre stole our remote control.'

The lady comes out of her house and walks over to us.

Bugger. I recognise her.

'I know you,' she says. 'You work at the gardening centre and you threw yourself across my husband's car when we were driving away, and you lay there for about 10 minutes, refusing to move.'

'Right, I'm ringing the police,' says Malcolm, but his voice is drowned out by an almighty clatter as all of the cuckoo clocks burst into life and deliver their sounds. What with the tv blaring out and cuckoo clocks singing, the noise is deafening.

'Time to go,' I say to Juan, and the two of us run like the wind.

Once we are back at my flat, we race into the sitting room and try to explain everything to Ted.

'And there were cookies, and the house was odd, then she gave us their remote control and the volume was too loud, and the cuckoo clocks went off, and the neighbour turned out to be this woman whose car I had laid on, so we ran. Just ran.'

'I don't understand any of that, Mary, but I'm very glad the police weren't called. Now, shouldn't you go and pack for our trip to Lapland tomorrow? And have you filled in all those forms they sent you, the ones asking for shoes sizes and things?'

'Yes, all done,' I say, as I go to fill them in. I'd completely forgotten all about them.

CHAPTER 13

22ND DECEMBER

'*D*o you ever think to yourself, *how on earth did I get here?*' asks Ted, as the taxi driver pulls up outside Gatwick airport.

'No, never. I think it's perfectly natural to be on a trip to Lapland to meet Father Christmas, all organised by David Beckham.'

Ted laughs and takes the bags out of the boot. 'I really don't know how you manage it, Mary Brown, but I'm very glad that you do.'

So, we're off. Brian and Oliver are travelling separately because they're flying from Scotland where Oliver has been having treatment at a hospital there, and we'll meet up with them tomorrow morning. For now, it's just Ted and me - off to a winter wonderland of pink skies, reindeer sleds, frosty fir trees, steaming hot chocolate and twinkling lights. And snow. Snow everywhere. I've been looking at videos of Lapland online and it's just a snow-filled fantasy. We are staying in the capital - Rovaniemi - which is perched on the edge of the Arctic Circle. Most importantly it's the official home of Father Christmas.

When we arrive in Lapland it's freezing cold. I realise that shouldn't come as a surprise to me: of course it's freezing. But I'm talking about a whole new level of cold here. So cold, in fact, that I'm wondering just how much wear I'm going to get out of the strappy sandals that I insisted on bringing, even though Ted said there was no point in bringing them because I wouldn't get any wear out of them. Damn it. I hate it when he's right.

It's also very dark even though it's only 3pm, so it's a struggle to see all the wondrous sights as we sit in the back of the taxi taking us to Santa Claus Holiday Village.

'You are here,' says the taxi driver. 'In the home of Father Christmas.'

'Thank you,' we both say as we clamber out of the warm car and move to collect our luggage from the boot.

'We will take care of that,' says a large blonde man with a huge beard. He looks like a Viking. He's also very attractive. And enormous. I see Ted standing up extra tall and puffing his chest out.

'I could look like that if I dyed my hair,' he says.

'Of course you could, dear.' I don't add that he'd also need to grow a few inches and spend the rest of his life in the gym.

Viking man tells us that his name is Martii. 'You have come on the shortest day of the year, which makes it a special day,' he says. 'But also, quite a cold and dark day. We have ski suits here for you to wear, to keep you warm.' A lady steps forward with ski suits. She must be about 20, she's tall, blonde and absolutely beautiful.

'That's more like it,' says Ted.

'Maybe come in here to change?' she says, leading us into the hotel reception and into a room just off the main hotel lobby. I try on the ski suit hoping to God that it fits. I find it so embarrassing when things don't fit me. I filled in that form last night and I said we both needed extra large sizes. Happily, the Laplandish extra-large is really big, so for the first time in my life I'm able to put on clothes which say they are extra-large and they turn out to be extra-large. If anything, mine are a bit too big. And you won't find me saying that very often.

We walk back into the lobby and Viking Man dazzles us with loads of interesting facts about the area, telling us that the line of the Arctic Circle runs right through the middle of the village. 'You can see it marked with a row of lanterns and blue lights,' he says in that lyrical, sing-song accent that makes me want to smile.

'Now I will take you on a reindeer sleigh ride so you can see some of it for yourselves.'

'Oh great,' I say, smiling warmly at Viking man. 'That would be lovely, thank you.'

'My very greatest pleasure.'

'I bet he takes steroids.' says Ted.

I jump onto Martii's sleigh (not a euphemism, sadly) and he takes us along the Forest Path, through fir trees piled up with snow as Ted and I snuggle up between blankets and reindeer hides. It' a wonderful, magical trip and I want it to go on and on. We don't see anyone else out in the snow as we skate along so gracefully that I feel like we're in another world altogether, or that the sleigh is going to lift into the air and glide through the late afternoon sky. Some of the journey takes us through large forests that look untouched except for the narrow trail we're on. It's wonderful.

'And here is house,' says Martii, pointing to a small cottage like something out of a fairy-tale. There's an elaborate wreath on the door, and you can see the Christmas tree inside, through the window, twinkling and welcoming.

'All your luggage is inside waiting for you.'

'Wow, thank you so much,' I say, as he helps me off the sleigh and puts his hand out to help Ted.

'I'm OK mate. Don't need any help, thanks.'

'Tonight, you may come to see the northern lights with me after Lappish food is delivered to your door. OK?'

'Oh yes, I'd love that,' I say while Ted shrugs and says he's heard the northern lights aren't that special.

'Will you behave, Ted?' I say, as we walk down the little path to our home for the next few days. 'Just because you don't like Viking man, doesn't mean you can spoil the whole trip.'

'Sorry, but he's a bit much, don't you think? Chucking compliments around and driving a bloody reindeer sleigh.'

'You might need to get into the spirit of the thing a bit more,' I say. 'If you think he's too much, I don't know what you're going to make of grown men and women dressed as elves and Santa Claus tomorrow.'

We've just unpacked and adjusted to our little home when there's a knock at the door and an old man with a long white beard hands us a box of food.

'We have put extra pancake,' says the man. 'Any more food needed, to call reception and I'll be back.'

'I'll be back,' says Ted, in the voice of Arnold Schwarzenegger, as he closes the door.

Inside the box there's a delicious soup with fresh salmon, a kind of pancake to go with the soup and some cookies with hot tea for dessert. We've just finished when there's another knock at the door.

'Blimey, we don't get this many visitors at home,' says Ted.

It's Viking Man. He has arrived to take us to see the northern lights.

'We will go now to try to see the lights. I can make no guarantees about this though,' Martii insists. 'It is a clear night, but you never know whether you will see them. We will go but I cannot promise.'

'We understand,' I say. Ted just shrugs. He seems to go quiet and sulky whenever Martii is around.

'The Northern Lights are also known as Aurora Borealis,' Viking man continues, and they are quite spectacularly beautiful. Very much like your girlfriend.'

I giggle like a schoolgirl at this. A handsome Viking who tells you you're spectacularly beautiful. What more could a girl want?

Ted just drops his head into his hands.

It takes a while before we see anything. I mean, it feels like we drive, walk and wait for ages but then a faint grey-green stripe becomes visible, soon becoming a vivid shot of green through the sky. In no time at all the sky looks like it's on fire, lit by green-purple flames. Green clouds of light now dance above us and all around us. I don't think I've ever seen anything quite so beautiful. It's entrancing, it makes you feel like you're being drawn in.

I'm staring up at it, mesmerised.

'Are you happy?' asks Ted, as we stand, wrapped around each other, watching the magnificent lights sweep through the skies.

'So happy. I'm the luckiest girl alive,' I say.

'No, I'm the lucky one,' says Ted. 'Look, there's something I want to ask you.'

'Sure.' I'm talking to Ted but my eyes are firmly fixed on the skies above us. When I eventually glance in his direction, he looks very serious.

'What is it? Is everything OK?'

'Mary - everything's perfect. It's been such a difficult year, with lockdown and us splitting up, then getting back together again. There were times when I thought I couldn't cope if we didn't get back together. I missed you so much when we were apart. I really love you.'

'Oh Ted. That's lovely.'

'I'd like us to take things to the next step.'

'How do you mean?'

'I think we should move in together.'

'Really? Oh my God, I'd love that.'

'If we both get rid of our flats, we can buy a place that's our own.'

'Oh wow. Wow. Ted, I'd love that so much.'

'So would I,' he says. 'I can't think of anything better, to be honest. I want to be with you for ever and ever'

'Oh, me too, Ted. Me too.'

And as I'm speaking, I'm standing in the snow with the northern lights dancing in the skies above me, as a large Viking claps and cheers at the news. I've thought a lot about Ted and I moving in together, but I never envisaged it being quite like this.

CHAPTER 14

23RD DECEMBER

'I'm so excited to meet Oliver,' I say to Ted, when we wake up, all snuggled up in our cosy bed.

'It's a shame he's only coming for two days though,' says Ted. 'I'd have thought they would have come early yesterday morning.'

'He's not well. His dad said that two days was the most he wanted to take him away for.'

'It must be really tough. I do feel for him.'

'I know I can't imagine how it must feel to have this lovely little boy who's got all these problems. And the fact that he's dealing with them all by himself. No mum to help share the worries and the joys.'

'Well, let's just make sure he has the best time possible while he's here,' says Ted, getting out of bed and waddling off to the shower. 'We're meeting them at 10 at that main hotel, so we should start getting ready.'

'I think Viking man is coming to pick us up and take us over there.'

'Oh, joy,' says Ted. 'Bloody wonderful.' Then his voice is drowned out by the sound of the shower. Once Ted has finished, I have a shower too. By 9.30, we're all dressed up in our padded ski suits, with bobble hats and gloves at the ready, waiting by our cottage door. But it's not Viking man who turns up to take us out for the day, it's an older man. He looks like a Viking too, to be honest, but nowhere near as big, hunky and handsome as yesterday's Nordic delight.

'I bet Martii didn't want to come,' says Ted. 'Now he knows we're going to move in together and he's got no chance with you.'

'Oh, Ted. Honestly, you are so ridiculous. As if a man like that wants anything to do with me anyway.'

'He said you were spectacularly beautiful. And he's right. But he shouldn't have said it.'

'He was just being kind. It's his job to make us feel good.'

'Well, he didn't make me feel very good when he was flirting with you.'

'Honestly, Ted, you are crackers sometimes.'

We head off to the hotel and as soon as we arrive, and I step off the snowmobile, I see Oliver. He looks just like his photo: incredibly pretty, big, blue eyes and this lovely pale blonde hair sticking out from beneath his furry hat.

'Hello, I'm Mary,' I say, clomping over to him in my big ski boots and waving like a lunatic. 'It's so lovely to meet you.'

His dad, Brian, has a lovely smile, like his son. He is quite a good looking in a scruffy sort of way; unshaven and tired looking with his hair all over the place. But I guess he's got his work cut out with this little one so it's understandable that he's not groomed to within an inch of his life.

I give Oliver a big hug. And then wonder whether I should have done that. Is he unstable? Is he unsteady on his feet? He doesn't seem to be. He just smiles and looks at me like he's not quite sure who I am. Brian shakes my hand and tells me that he cannot begin to thank me enough for organising all this.

'Really, it's no problem,' I tell him.

'We saw lovely dogs, didn't we dad?' says Oliver.

'We did son,' replies Brian.

'We went on a husky ride when we arrived yesterday evening. It was all a bit terrifying. But good fun.'

'Oh my god, that sounds amazing. I'm so glad you got to do that. We had a reindeer ride, which was really lovely as well, but probably not quite as adrenaline surging as the Husky ride.'

'We went faster than the wind,' says Oliver, swinging his arms from side to side to show me the speed at which they travelled. And you know who we're going to meet now don't you?'

'Well, I've heard a rumour, but I'm not sure whether it's true,' I say

'We're seeing Father Christmas,' whispers Oliver, conspiratorially. 'In his Grotto, which is where he lives. Are you coming as well?'

'I am coming and I'm really looking forward to it. I hope you've been good so you get lots of presents.'

'I'm always good,' says Oliver. 'The only time I'm not good is when I'm bad.'

We all laugh at this. He's a lovely kid. I'm so glad I could do this for him. He seems to be having the time of his life.

We climb on to the snowmobile that is taking us over to Santa's Grotto, and I sit next to Oliver, while Ted and Brian sit behind us. Oliver is lovely company. He even tells me about his leg, and how he only has one, and has to wear a false leg.

'I'll show you later if you like, but I can't show you now because it's in my ski suit that's tucked into my boot, and I can't get to it.'

'That's okay. I think you should keep your ski suit all tucked in to keep you nice and warm.'

'You've got to keep nice and warm when it's snowing and cold like this, haven't you?'

'Oh, you have,' I confirm. 'I nearly forgot to bring my hat. My head would have been very cold, wouldn't it?'

Oliver laughs, then he tells me that he would have lent me his hat if I'd forgotten mine. I give him a warm hug before we fall into a rather peaceful, comfortable silence, looking out at the huge fir trees painted thickly with snow and the signs telling us we're approaching Santa's grotto. I hear Ted and Brian chatting companionably behind us as we zoom along. Lovely Ted is asking him how he copes, and how difficult it must be to do this all alone.

I hear Brian telling him that it's hard, but worth it. He says he'd love to meet someone, and have a relationship, but he doesn't see how it would be possible.

'I'd have to meet a very special woman who would be kind and thoughtful enough to give me the space to spend time with Oliver when I need to. I just don't think it's going to happen while Ollie is so young.'

I hear the words, without really thinking about them, but then a thought bursts into my mind.

And I think you know what that thought is: Belinda.

How great would that be?

Belinda is kind and thoughtful, and would be perfect for Brian.

Quite how I'm going to bring this subject up with him, and ask him whether I can make an introduction, is something I can't quite get my head round at the moment, but bring it up I must because this, Ladies and Gentlemen, might be the kindest thing I could do for this man and his lovely son.

We arrive at Santa's grotto, and are greeted by elves who put down the toys they are making in Santa's amazing toy factory, and rush to help us off the sleigh.

If they're surprised to discover there's only one child on the sleigh, they manage to hide it, and treat us all to a charming welcome. It's all beautifully choreographed with dancers and singers and elves cavorting in the snow. But I'm not sure I want to go in and meet Santa, and I know that Ted won't want to.

'I think I might be a bit too big to sit on Santa's lap,' he says. 'Fancy some of that gluhwein over there?'

There's a stall, on the far side, dishing out a rather pungent-smelling hot alcoholic drink. And it feels like the best thing we could do for ourselves at 11am, so we stroll over, sit on the bench and sip away. It's lovely there, snuggled up to Ted, being warmed by love and alcohol.

Oliver emerges later, squealing with delight and hugging the biggest teddy bear I've ever seen. His father carries a separate box with a train set in it - something that Oliver has always wanted.

'I'm so excited,' says Oliver. 'I can't wait to show my friends.'

'We're going down to the children's party now. Do you want to come?' asks Brian, but he already knows the answer, and smiles when I tell him that we're just going to spend a bit of time here, then head back to the hotel and have a look around the area.

'We'll catch up with you later,' I say, as they head off, marching through the snow with their gifts.

In the end we don't catch up with them that day: they roll from party to event, as they're taken around to meet everyone, and given the best possible treatment that can be given to a five-year-old boy. Ted and I have a rather more grown-up time going out to dinner at a beautiful restaurant.

24th December:

The next morning, we have breakfast alone together before catching up with Oliver and Brian to fly back home. I've got one last surprise for Oliver...the fact that David Beckham will be at the airport to meet him. We've already established that he's a big David Beckham fan so I'm hoping he'll be thrilled by the surprise.

At the airport, Ted takes Oliver for a walk around while I sit quietly with Brian. I'm not quite sure how to bring this up, but I'm absolutely determined to. 'Look', I say eventually. 'I'm sorry this is a bit embarrassing, but I've got this lovely friend who's single and dying to meet someone. Do you mind if I give her your number? You know, put the two of you in touch?'

'Gosh. Really? I'm not sure anyone would want to take on someone like me.'

'I think Belinda would love to take on someone like you.'

'Oh, OK. Tell me a bit about her.'

I put her name into Google to call up her picture on the

company website, but when I google her name, the picture that comes up is of her at dinner with Ted at the fake date that went wrong.

'Oh, is that her there? But isn't that Ted?'

'Yes, it's a rather long story. I won't bore you with the details but - yes - that's her having lunch with my boyfriend.'

Brian looks unsure.

'She's a sweet, lovely person. I think you'd like her a lot.'

'Okay. Okay. Go on, let's give it a go,' says Brian, handing me my phone back.

'Brilliant,' I say, as we board the plane and prepare to head home for Christmas. 'I'll fix something up once we're back.'

I sit next to Ted on the flight home, and we spend much of the time talking about what sort of place we're going to get.

'Will you promise me something,' says Ted, as the pilot announces that we're coming in to land. 'Don't make any plans for tonight. We've had a madly busy week, and we're visiting family tomorrow and for the whole of next week. It's Christmas Eve and I'd like the two of us to be home together for once. Alone. OK?'

'Of course,' I say. 'That would be lovely.'

We arrive back at Gatwick airport and the four of us are taken aside, and told there is someone to meet us.

Brian looks a little concerned, then out walks David Beckham causing Oliver to squeal, then Ted squeals and then Brian squeals. I just say 'Hi David, how lovely to see you again' and - I swear to God - I feel like the coolest person ever to walk the earth.

David chats to Oliver and gives him piles of presents, including signed football shirts and tracksuits and some amazing computer games. I stand on the edge of it all, watching with pride, but also staring at David's bottom in what could be described as an inappropriate manner.

As Oliver and David chat, my phone rings. I answer the call and hear Keith's dulcet tones on the other end. I assume he's calling to find out how the trip went, but he sounds like he's in a disco.

'Where on earth are you?' I say.

'I'm at work. Rick Astley's just turned up and he's entertaining the crowds.'

'What?'

'Yes - he saw the Rick Astley decorations on the Christmas trees when the blind date feature was in the paper, and he came down to meet you. Hurry back.'

I look over at Ted, sitting there on his own, patiently waiting for me.

'Actually, I won't. I'm going to head home now, but have a lovely Christmas, and please thank Rick for me, and get lots of pictures of him in front of the Rick Astley decorated tree, OK?'

'Are you serious?' says Keith. 'This is Rick Astley. He's just about to sing 'Never Gonna Give You Up'.'

'It sounds great, Keith. Have a lovely evening. I'll see you next year.'

I smile at Ted. 'Let's go,' I say. 'We've got a whole, wonderful future to plan.'

ENDS...for now...

What will happen next? Will they move in with one another? Will things go smoothly? Or will Mary find something of Ted's that shocks her so much that she is forced to re-think whether they should be moving in together at all?And what about Belinda's date with Brian?

See: Adorable Fat Girl on Valentine's Day... COMING IN FEBRUARY in ebook, paperback and audiobook!

My Book

CPSIA information can be obtained
at www.ICGtesting.com
Printed in the USA
LVHW051502290321
682830LV00040B/2957